D141961A

USBORNE

SANDY
LANE
STABLES

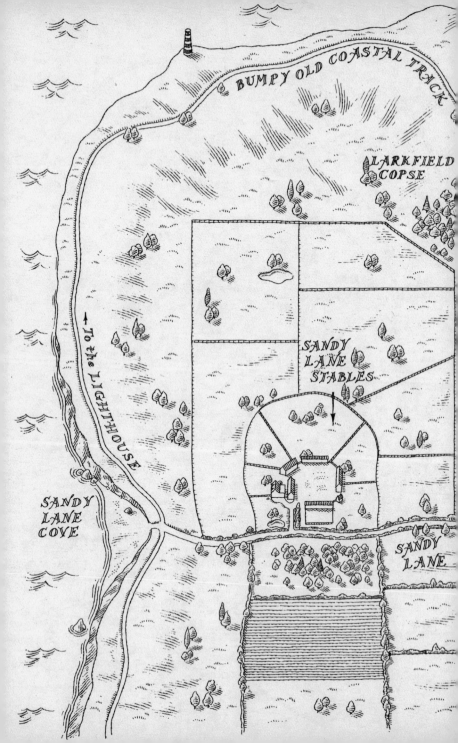

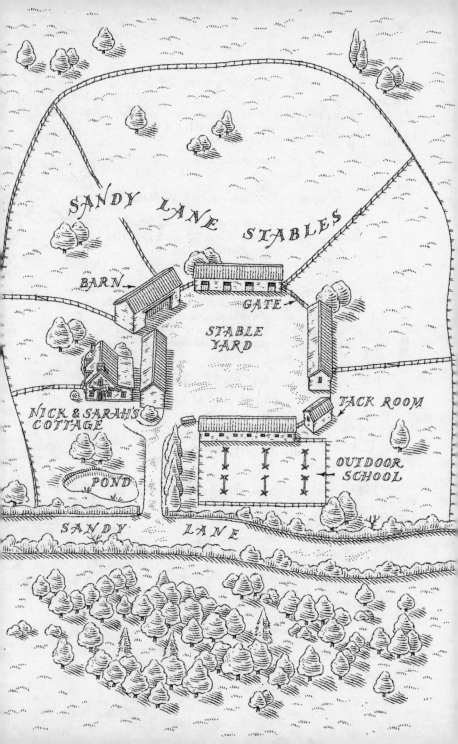

First published in 1998 by Usborne Publishing Ltd,
Usborne House, 83-85 Saffron Hill, London
EC1N 8RT, England.

www.usborne.com

A catalogue record for this title is available from
the British Library

ISBN 07460 3329 X (paperback)
ISBN 07460 3330 3 (hardback)

Typeset in Times

Printed in Great Britain

Series Editor: Gaby Waters
Editors: Cecily Von Ziegesar and Susannah Leigh
Designer: Lucy Parris
Cover photograph supplied by: Bob Langrish
Map illustrations by John Woodcock

THE PERFECT PONY

Michelle Bates

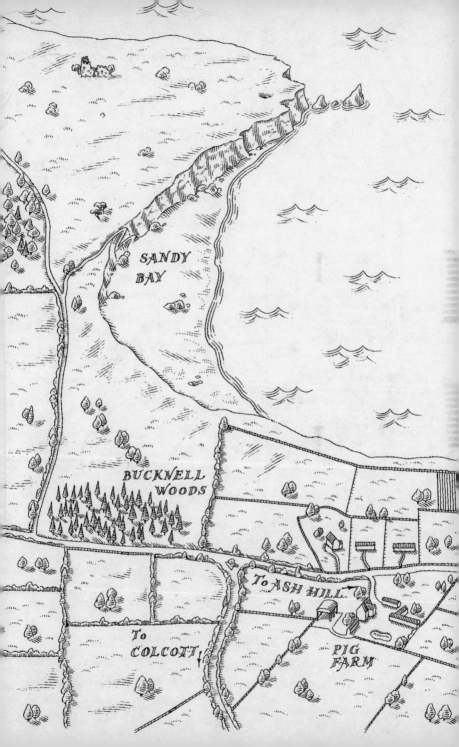

SANDY
BAY

BUCKNELL
WOODS

To ASH HILL

To
COLCOTT

PIG
FARM

CONTENTS

1

PONIES AND CRICKET!

"There must be *something* I can do to raise the money. What about a car washing business? I could charge a fiver a car!" Alex Hardy followed his sister in and out of each of the stables at Sandy Lane.

"Sounds great," Kate answered, but Alex could tell she wasn't really listening. "Look, can you help fill these water buckets," she went on. "The horses will be back from the ride any minute. They'll be thirsty."

"Yeah, yeah all right. On second thoughts, maybe car washing isn't such a good idea," Alex said. "There's that new garage opened over by Colcott. It's got a spray jet *and* it's only £3 a go."

"Look, Alex." Kate stopped still in her tracks and put down her water bucket. "If I hear you go on about the money for this cricket tour one more time I'll go mad!" She scooped up her long, blond hair and tied it into a pony tail. It was a warm summer's evening, and she was looking hot and bothered. "I couldn't care less if you robbed a bank to get the money." She picked up her bucket and went into the next stable.

"Robbed a bank? Now that's a thought!" Alex's eyes flashed as he followed her.

"What are all the other boys doing?" Kate asked.

"Will's doing a sponsored parachute jump, Harry's organizing a roller-blading evening, oh, and Jim's working at Thorne Park for the summer."

"A lot more exciting than car-washing!" Kate exclaimed.

"I guess you're right," Alex said, feeling frustrated. The more he thought about it, the less likely it seemed he'd get to go on the cricket tour to South Africa.

"When do you need to get the money by, anyway?" Kate asked.

"15th October," Alex replied.

"And how much is it you need?" Kate asked.

"Another £350," Alex said gloomily. "The whole trip's £850. Mum and Dad said I could use the money I won on that premium bond, but getting the other £350 isn't going to be easy."

"You're lucky Mum and Dad are letting you spend the money," Kate said. "I thought you were supposed to be saving that for university."

"Yeah I know, but they realize how important this tour is," Alex shrugged.

"It sounds more like a holiday if you ask me," Kate muttered under her breath. "Hang on, I've got an idea." Kate's eyes lit up. "Maybe you *could* make this money. Maybe you could organize a sponsored ride. We made loads last time we did one of those. You could do something a bit different – like making it fancy dress or something."

Alex groaned and made a face. "Too girly."

"I might have known I'd get a comment like that from an older brother – where's your imagination?" Kate raised her eyebrows.

But Alex wasn't paying any attention. "What if I sold my stereo?" he murmured.

"What that clapped-out heap of junk?" Kate laughed. "Who's going to buy that?"

"If you're not going to make any helpful comments, don't bother," Alex stormed.

"Oh Alex, look, I'll have a think about it later, OK?" Kate shoved a bundle of hay into one of the nets. "Right now I have to sort out these ponies – and you said you'd help me."

"All right, don't nag." Alex brushed his messy, brown hair out of his eyes. "Where shall I start?"

"You could *start* by filling up the rest of the water buckets. Then Pepper and Blackjack need grooming. They're lame at the moment, so they haven't gone out on the ride. Oh and Hector's about too."

"OK, I get the picture," Alex moaned. The work seemed never-ending. There was always some job to be done at Sandy Lane. Where were the rest of the regular Sandy Lane riders when they were needed? Tom, Rosie, Jess – all of them used the stables more than he did these days. The only reason he was here at all this evening was because his cricket practice had been cancelled and Kate had bullied him into it. It wasn't that he disliked being at Sandy Lane – a few years ago, you wouldn't have found him anywhere else. But there were other things that took up his time now – things that he was better at anyway – football, tennis, and now cricket. Ever since he'd been selected for the junior county squad there just hadn't been any time for riding.

"Did you get all that?" Kate said.

Alex didn't have a chance to answer his sister before she dashed off across the yard. He watched her disappear into the tack room. Kate hadn't stopped since they'd got there, but then horses had always been her number one priority.

Bending down, Alex picked up a couple of buckets, and made his way across the yard to the water trough. As he turned on the hose, his mind went back to the problem of the money. He just had to get on that tour. He was so busy thinking that he didn't notice the water rise to the top of the bucket and start spilling over.

"Oh blast." Alex jumped out of the way and turned off the hose. The buckets were full to the brim. Tightly gripping the handles, he walked across the yard and slipped into Pepper's stable. He deposited a bucket with the little piebald pony and then he made his way into Hector's stable.

"All right in here?" Alex clapped Hector's solid, brown shoulder and put the other water bucket down on the ground. Hector started slurping greedily. At

4

16.2 hands, Hector was the largest horse in the yard and, though some riders complained that he was stubborn, Alex liked him the best. He was solid and stable – not like some of the more flighty mounts. Alex gave Hector a quick rub-down and ran the body brush over his back. As he bent down to pick out Hector's feet, he heard the crunch of hooves on the gravel and the sound of excited voices. Alex looked out over the stable door. The ride was back and Nick Brooks, the owner of the stables, was dishing out instructions.

"How are you getting on, Alex?" Kate called across to him from Feather's stable.

"Not bad. I've filled the water buckets *and* I've almost finished grooming Hector," Alex answered, drawing back the bolt and stepping out into the yard.

"Is that all?" Kate cried. "I've groomed Pepper and Blackjack *and* filled all the haynets!"

"Oh no, it's not a competition, is it?" Alex rolled his eyes.

"I've missed hearing the Hardys argue." Nick grinned as he walked over to where Alex was still standing. "Hello stranger. Haven't seen you around much. How's it going?"

"Not bad... not bad at all," Alex said nonchalantly. "Just thought I'd come and lend a hand down here tonight."

"Great!" Nick scratched his head. "So what's the news? I hear you've made the county cricket squad."

"Well, just the junior side," Alex replied. "What's been going on here?"

"Oh, the usual," Nick answered. "Kate's probably told you about Pepper and Blackjack going lame, and I'm afraid we've had a bit of a crisis this afternoon as well. Minstrel took a kick to his right foreleg out on the hack. I've had to call the vet out."

"What's this?" Kate called, having overheard half the conversation. "Who's injured?" She walked over to join the group.

"Minstrel." Nick nodded back across the yard. "He got kicked this afternoon. It's quite a deep cut."

"Oh no!" Kate looked worried. "So Sandy Lane's three horses down now."

"I know, it's not good news," Nick said despondently. "I've been trying to think of ways of replacing the ponies. I don't want to buy any as Pepper and Blackjack will only be out of action for about a month. Still, we'll just have to manage. So you guys break up from school tomorrow, right?" he said, changing the subject. "I expect you're looking forward to it."

"You bet," Alex answered him. "Six weeks of freedom."

Nick laughed.

"And Izzy'll be back from boarding school this weekend," Kate joined in. "It'll be good to see her."

"Yes – she's booked Midnight in at Sandy Lane from Sunday," Nick said. "So at least we'll be able to use him in lessons."

Izzy was Kate's best friend. She'd been at boarding school for a year now, and her horse, Midnight, had gone with her. When she came back for the holidays, she stabled him at Sandy Lane and Nick used him at the yard in return for his board.

"Why don't you two head off home now?" Nick suggested. "You'll be spending enough of the holidays here as it is, Kate, and I can finish up tonight."

"Are you sure?" Kate asked.

"Positive," Nick replied. "You're around on Saturday, aren't you?"

"Definitely." A big grin spread across Kate's face.

"Good," said Nick. "I thought I might find time to give you and Feather a bit of training in the outdoor school – by way of a thank you for all the extra work you've put in here lately."

"Really? That would be great!" Kate said.

"We've got high hopes for you and Feather this summer." Nick looked across at the little grey pony. "If you don't come back with a bunch of rosettes from the shows there's going to be trouble."

"I get the hint," Kate grinned. "Are you ready, Alex?" She turned to her brother.

"Yup," Alex answered, getting onto his bike. "All set."

"So will you be around on Saturday too, Alex?" Nick asked.

"Well, I don't know; I've got a lot of cricket practices now," Alex said. "But we'll see."

And with that, Alex and Kate cycled out of the yard, leaving Nick waving them off at the front gate.

2

THE PERFECT SOLUTION

"Hmm, three lame ponies is bad news." Kate looked thoughtful. "I wonder what Nick'll do." She spread a thick layer of peanut butter over her piece of toast and took a bite.

Alex pushed back the kitchen bench and got up from the table. Feeling disgruntled, he looked out of the window of the converted mill where they lived, and out onto the darkening garden.

"I hope it won't mean Feather'll get over-worked in lessons now," Kate frowned. "I know it's selfish, but I'd sort of been hoping Nick might ease up on using her now that I'm training her."

"So I take it you haven't had any great ideas then?" Alex started.

"What?" Kate looked puzzled, and then a dawning

realization crossed her face. "Oh Alex, you're not still going on about this cricket tour, are you?" she said, burying her head in a pony magazine.

"Yes, believe it or not, I am." Alex picked up the local paper and started flicking through it. A new dog rescue centre, the local swimming club, St. Michael's Church bazaar – nothing much of interest. What was on at the cinema?

Alex turned to the back pages and, as he looked down one of the columns, an announcement caught his eye. Alex stopped for a moment.

"Here, Kate. Take a look at this."

"What?" Kate glanced over to where Alex was stabbing the paper with his finger.

"The Ash Hill Sale, Saturday 17th July." She read the words aloud. "So what?"

"So I think I just might have got an idea," Alex said excitedly.

"Uh oh," Kate frowned. "Why do I suddenly get the feeling I'm not going to like it?"

"Like it?" Alex sat back down beside her. "You're going to love it. It's not just an idea, it's a brainwave! I might just have solved all of my problems – and Sandy Lane's – in one easy go."

"Go on," Kate said.

"Sponsored rides, car-washing... what rubbish ideas – the answer was staring me in the face. Why didn't I open this paper before? I'm going to buy a pony."

"A pony!" Kate looked perplexed. "Why?"

"Well, it'll help Nick and Sarah out for starters,"

Alex said, drumming his fingers on the table.

"And?" Kate asked.

"And it's the perfect way of making that extra £350," Alex grinned. "I buy a pony. Nick and Sarah use it. In the mean time, it gets trained up and I can sell it on for a profit at the end of the summer. I get the rest of the money for my tour and – there you go – everyone's happy."

"Hey, not so fast," Kate said. " Mum and Dad might say you can spend the premium bond money on a cricket tour, but they're not going to let you spend it on a pony."

"Well, I won't tell them," Alex said simply. "Not until I've made the money anyway. Then – hey presto – I'll announce I can go to South Africa and they'll be as proud as anything."

"Well, I don't know." Kate looked doubtful. "How do you know you'll definitely be able to make a profit anyway? You know as well as I do that ponies are the most unpredictable of creatures. They're..." She searched for the word.

"But if Nick's training it, it'll be all right," Alex interrupted. "Look at Storm Cloud. She turned out great, didn't she?"

"Storm Cloud's different," Kate said firmly, thinking about Sandy Lane's star pony, bought at the Ash Hill Sale. She'd arrived at the stables a complete mess, but Nick had nursed her back to health. "She had real promise – anyone could see that. Look Alex, buying from a sale isn't exactly safe, is it? You don't know what you're getting."

"No, but at least I'll know what I'm doing," Alex said. "I've been to Ash Hill with Uncle Jack so many times, haven't I?"

"Yes, I guess you have," Kate replied.

Their Uncle Jack was a bloodstock agent over on the other side of Walbrook. Alex had spent the summer before last working for him.

"But what about looking after this pony?" Kate looked thoughtful.

"If it lived at Sandy Lane it could be just another of the ponies. It could be looked after by whoever's about." Alex wrinkled up his forehead.

"And what about its food?"

"It can live off the summer grass," Alex answered promptly. "I'll sell it on before the winter so I won't have to pay for extra feed. See? I've got it all thought out. It's a brilliant plan, isn't it?"

"Well, I reckon that Nick would be pleased with the help," Kate said slowly. "Maybe it is a good idea. It beats car-washing anyway. See what Mum and Dad say."

Alex grinned, totally taken up with his idea.

"So what are you going to look for?" Kate asked.

"I'm not quite sure," Alex said. "You could help me decide..."

*

11

"You should be doing this for yourself, Alex," Kate said crossly as she flicked through the Ash Hill Sale catalogue on Friday evening.

"I know, but I value your opinion," Alex wheedled, not paying the least bit of attention as he sat in front of the TV and flicked through the channels.

"More like you can't be bothered to read all the small print," Kate growled.

Alex shrugged. "Go on, admit it, Kate. You like doing it. You can't resist taking a look."

"You're right," Kate agreed. "Anything to do with horses interests me which is more than can be said for you just sitting there. You'll have to check with Nick and Sarah that it's OK."

"All right," Alex interrupted her. "Now how are you getting on with the catalogue?"

"Well, " Kate took a deep breath. "This grey pony here sounds all right – lot number 60, and then there's this dun pony here – lot number 52. Ooh, and there's a nice-sounding brown pony."

"Enough... enough." Alex raised his hand in the air. "I said a couple of suggestions... not every pony in the catalogue."

"OK, OK," Kate giggled. "Here you go. I've put a cross by the ones I like. I'm sure you'll be able to get one of those. You do know what you're doing, Alex, don't you?"

"Of course I do." Alex looked faintly irritated. "It'll be fine. What could possibly go wrong?"

3

THE ASH HILL SALE

Alex rolled over in bed on Saturday morning and stretched out his arms. It was going to be a warm day and he was excited at the thought of getting into the thick of things at Ash Hill. He wouldn't have to check what he was doing with Uncle Jack either as he was spending his own money. Alex jumped out of bed and scrambled into his clothes. He'd already taken the cash out of his building society account – all £500 of it – and he was ready for action.

Kate was at the breakfast table ahead of him and his mother stood at the hob.

"You're just in time for some bacon and eggs," Mrs. Hardy said. "I'm not going to be making it for you every day, but I thought I'd give you a treat on the first morning of the holidays."

"Thanks Mum." Alex took the plate of food that

she offered and sat down at the kitchen table.

"Right Kate, shall we be off?" Mrs. Hardy turned to her daughter.

"Where are you going?" Alex munched his way through a mouthful of food.

"The stables," Kate answered him.

"I said I'd give Kate a lift on my way into Colcott," Mrs. Hardy explained. "What are your plans for the day?"

"Oh, cricket and stuff," Alex said vaguely.

Mrs. Hardy nodded. "Kate darling – I'll just get my sunglasses from upstairs, then we'll be off."

"All right, Mum." Kate stood waiting as her mother disappeared out of the room.

"You don't fancy coming to the sale with me, do you?" Alex said.

"I can't," Kate groaned. "Nick said he'd give Feather and me some extra training. I thought you were OK about going on your own."

"I am, I am. I just thought it would be nice to have some company," Alex grumbled. "Forget it."

"Shall we go?" Mrs. Hardy appeared in the kitchen and then she turned to her son. "Can you put the burglar alarm on if you go out."

"Sure," Alex answered.

"All right, we're off." Mrs. Hardy turned to her daughter.

Alex waited for a few minutes after he heard the car start up before he got to his feet. There was no point in hanging around inside. Grabbing a sweatshirt, he punched in the numbers on the alarm and slipped

14

out of the front door. As he walked down the road to the bus stop, he patted the pocket of his jeans where he'd stashed his envelope full of cash. The bus to Ash Hill rumbled around the corner, and Alex felt a rush of adrenaline flood through him. Whistling to himself, he climbed aboard, scrabbling around in his pockets for some loose change. The bus set off, rattling around the winding roads, and Alex sat down. 9 o'clock – plenty of time to get to the sale and look round before it started at ten.

Alex was feeling pretty confident. Wait till Nick saw the pony that evening... wait till all the others saw it too. They'd be pretty impressed with him. Fleetingly Alex remembered he hadn't actually mentioned his idea to Nick, but as he was giving them the use of a pony, what could be the problem? Anyway, it would be a nice surprise.

Soon they were rumbling through the countryside, passing woods and fields, until they neared the outskirts of Ash Hill. As they reached the corner of Warmouth Road, Alex rang the bell and the bus jolted to a halt. He jumped down and walked back down the road to the sale ground.

It was busy as he walked through the wrought iron gates. The courtyard was bursting with people, and horses were being led this way and that.

Alex looked at the catalogue. First things first – he'd check out the ponies Kate had marked – a dun, two browns and a grey. Flicking through the catalogue, he came to the first of them. "Lot number 43, registered working dun pony." He read the words out loud. "Rising four, two white socks, 13 hands, without shoes, fully warranted."

Alex walked into the building housing the horses and ponies. People were milling around as Alex made his way up and down each of the aisles in search of the dun pony. As he came to it, he cast a critical eye over its back. It looked all right, but nothing to get enthusiastic about. He gave it a tick and moved on. The two brown ponies weren't far away, and once Alex had given them a cursory glance, he gave them a tick too. It was just the grey now. Alex battled his way through the crowds, trying to make his way to where she was tied. He could just about see the top of her head, but there were so many people around, there wasn't time for much more. He really ought to see the four ponies led out in hand to check they were sound. Uncle Jack always did – but then Uncle Jack was a bit fussy like that.

Alex fanned himself with the catalogue – it was pretty hot and stuffy in here. As he walked out of the building and over to the ringside, he stopped by the refreshments van.

"Can of lemonade please." He handed over the money and looked at his watch, feeling excited at the thought of bidding against everyone else. He really ought to go and register his name – the dun pony wouldn't be in for a while yet, but the sale had already started. Alex squeezed his way through the jostling crowds to the registration kiosk.

"Name and address?" the woman behind the counter asked.

"Alex Hardy. The Old Mill, Priory Lane, Colcott," he said confidently, grabbing the numbered card that was pushed towards him. He was glad he was so tall – she hadn't even queried his age. Registration number 64. Alex looked down at the card as he made his way to the building housing the ring where the horses would be sold. He squeezed through the rows of people and found a spot on the right just as a bay mare was being led into the ring.

"Lot number 22... what will you give me for this horse here? Who'll start me at £150?" The auctioneer's voice sounded muffled over the loud-speaker. A man on the right of the ring raised his hand and the auctioneer nodded. "150, I'm bid. 200?"

Alex watched another man raise his hand in the air and again the auctioneer acknowledged it, and now the bidding was speeding up.

"250, 300, 400... " The auctioneer was going so fast that Alex could hardly hear what was going on. At £500, the auctioneer brought his hammer down on the desk in front of him with a loud bang. The mare had been sold and was being led out of the ring.

Alex watched another ten horses led in and out of the ring. It wasn't long before the working dun pony was brought in. The pony looked on his toes and danced eagerly at the end of his lead rope. Alex waited for the bidding to start. £200... £300... Alex cast his eyes this way and that, itching to put in a bid. But before he knew it, the price was already up to £450. In the blink of an eye, the pony was sold for £600. Alex hadn't even had the chance to raise his hand.

Oh well, that pony had been out of his price range anyway. He felt a little twinge of doubt that it wasn't going to be as easy as he thought.

"Are you here to buy something?" The lady standing next to him tapped him on the shoulder.

"Yes, yes I am," Alex answered.

"Well, you have to be pretty quick off the mark if you're going to bid," she said kindly.

"Oh I know," Alex said, feeling faintly irritated that he must have looked as though he didn't know what he was doing.

"Well, good luck," the lady smiled as she walked away.

Alex settled back down to watch another twenty or so lots led in and out of the ring. When the first of the brown ponies was brought in, Alex was ready to hit the bidding. As the price reached £400, he raised his hand.

"400, I'm bid," the auctioneer called, and Alex felt pleased with himself. But the feeling was only momentary. Soon the bidding had jumped to £450 and then £500 and he was out of the running again.

"Sold... sold for £700," the words of the auctioneer finally rang out.

Head down, Alex flicked through the catalogue. There were another fifty or so lots till the next brown pony. Alex decided he'd go and get some fresh air. Slowly he ambled outside and over to the refreshments van.

"Cheese roll please." Alex fumbled around in his pocket for the money.

The man handed it over and Alex unwrapped the roll, looking around him. People were drifting around as the loudspeaker relayed the ponies' prices. Alex threw the wrapper into a bin and made his way back to the ringside. It wasn't long now until the next brown pony. Alex looked down at his catalogue. The estimate was £450, so it was already at the top end of what he had to spend.

Two more horses were sold, and then the brown pony was led in. The bidding quickly rose to £200, and Alex joined in. In no time at all it went to £300... then £400 and soon it was way past £500. Not again. Alex felt frustrated – yet another pony had gone for more money than he'd expected.

Alex gritted his teeth. The grey was only a few lots away now. One horse... two horses... three horses... sold.

Impatiently he waited until the grey pony was led into the ring. Was it his imagination, or was the pony limping? This was crazy. As the pony was led around, the bidding got faster and faster until Alex's head was reeling.

£200... £300... £400. What if the pony wasn't sound? He was too scared to bid in case it wasn't. And then the hammer had come crashing down again – this time at £500 – and yet another pony was led out of the ring. Alex took a deep breath. He just had to get a pony that day.

"Lot number 145. £200... who'll give me £200 for this pony?" The words of the auctioneer rang out into the crowd. Alex craned his neck around the people in front of him to look into the ring. There were so many people in front of him that he couldn't get a clear view of the pony. Still, what he could see looked OK – as good as any of the others. Why not put in a bid?

No one had bid anything yet, so maybe he was in with a chance. At £200, Alex raised his hand. His eyes flashed around the ring, daring anyone to out-bid him. A burly-looking man across the wayside raised his hand at £300, and Alex nodded at £400. Things were hotting up now and Alex was in the thick of it. He couldn't go much higher. There – £500 – that was his limit.

Alex's face flushed as he realized all eyes were upon him. He was just about to leave when he noticed that the crowd had hushed. He looked over to the opposite side of the ring to where the other man had been bidding, but he was turning away now to talk to his friend.

"Go-in-g... go-in-g... go-ne." The hammer dropped and Alex panicked. What had he done? He hadn't even looked at the pony properly. The man next to him nudged his elbow, and Alex realized they were waiting for his registration number. Shakily, Alex raised the numbered card in the air, just as the pony was being led out of the ring.

Try to keep calm, Alex said to himself. *It'll be all right.* Quickly, he turned to the catalogue and scrabbled through it.

"Lot number 145... number 145," he muttered under his breath as he ran his finger down the typewritten pages until he came to the entry.

"Chestnut mare: Puzzle, 14 hands." He read the words aloud, hardly conscious of the people around him. "Much-loved. Competed locally at shows. Sadly outgrown."

There was no warranty, but the pony sounded all right. There... Alex breathed a sigh of relief. That sounded OK. He'd go and pay for the pony and get everything sorted out. Patting his breast pocket to check the money was still there, he made his way over to the kiosk.

"Yes?" a woman's voice came from behind the counter as Alex hit the head of the queue.

"Yes, I've just bought a pony and I'd like to pay for it."

"Which lot?" the woman said.

"Lot number 145," Alex started, fumbling around in his pockets for the envelope of cash.

"Come on," an impatient voice came from behind him.

"Just one moment," Alex said, handing over a bundle of ten pound notes.

"Do you want to have the pony delivered somewhere?" the woman asked.

"Yes, er, that'll be great. It needs to go to the other side of Colcott," Alex answered.

"That'll be £15."

"Well, um." Alex stumbled over the words, knowing full well that he'd only got £5 left. "Actually, I don't really need a box."

"Show your receipt to the man over there and you'll

be free to take her," the woman answered.

Alex looked down at his receipt. The woman behind the counter was already onto the next customer as he made his way across the courtyard. Hurriedly, he handed over the slip of paper to the man waiting, and then Alex was shown down rows and rows of ponies, until finally he arrived at the back of the chestnut pony.

"Here you are – this one's yours." The man pointed and disappeared off down the aisle, leaving Alex at the pony's backside. The pony was roped into a sort of pen and facing the wall, so Alex couldn't really see her at first. He slipped under the rope, careful to avoid her hindquarters, and stepped alongside her shoulder.

"Hello there," Alex muttered, taking a good look at what he'd bought. Alex patted her neck, but he didn't get much of a response. He cast a critical eye over her and a wave of disgust flooded through him. She was filthy. Deep patches of mud clung in whorls on her shaggy chestnut coat and her red-brown mane, knotted and tangled, hung over her eyes. As Alex looked a bit closer he realized the pony was so thin you could almost see the ribs through her coat. Still, she'd be all right once she was cleaned up and had a good feed.

Alex untied the pony's rope, thinking back to the words used to describe her in the catalogue. *'Much-loved, sadly outgrown'* – what a joke!

As Alex led her out across the dirty floor he wasn't really sure what he should do. He hadn't got enough money to get her boxed anywhere. Alex thought hard. Kate would still be at Sandy Lane now. He'd give her a call.

Slowly he led the pony out of the building. No one even batted an eyelid as he crossed the courtyard and made his way to the exit. Alex tied the pony up to some railings and hurried over to the public phone box. He slotted in a coin and dialled the number for Sandy Lane, twisting the phone cord in his hands while he waited for someone to answer.

"Come on, come on," he muttered as the phone rang at the other end.

At last someone picked up the receive. It was a voice he didn't recognize.

"Oh hello, is Kate Hardy around? It's Alex.. yes, her brother."

Alex waited and then Kate's breathless voice sounded at the other end.

"Alex... what's the matter?" she asked.

"Kate, can you come to Ash Hill? Yes, now. Please. Don't ask any questions... just come. Meet me at the left of the front entrance, and bring a grooming kit. It's really important."

Alex put down the phone and walked to where he'd tied up the pony. Sandy Lane wasn't far from Ash Hill so it shouldn't take Kate long on the bus. He took another glance at the pony – she really wasn't much to look at. Still, a pony didn't have to be pretty to be useful. The sooner he got her settled at Sandy Lane, the sooner his plan would be in motion.

4

A DEAL IS STRUCK

Alex stood up from where he was sitting and stretched his legs. An hour had passed since he'd phoned Kate. Where had she got to? He was tired of waiting. Alex waved a hand in front of the pony's eyes, but she didn't so much as flicker an eyelid.

"Come on, you rotten thing. You could at least acknowledge I'm here," Alex said crossly.

"Alex... Alex..."

Alex looked up to see Kate, sprinting down the road towards him.

"Did you buy a pony? Where is it? Why the terrible hurry?" Her words came out in short staccato sentences, her eyes darting this way and that. She didn't even register the little pony and with a sinking heart, Alex realized that Kate was obviously expecting him to get a bit more for his money.

"It's over there?" Alex grunted and pointed to where the pony was standing.

"There?" And, as Kate realized that he was pointing at the little chestnut pony in front of her, she turned and stared at him in disbelief.

"What? This New Forest pony here? You mean... you've bought *this* pony?"

Alex nodded.

"But she's... I mean, she's..." Kate looked bewildered. "Well, she's so thin. She looks ill. Oh you poor little thing." She stroked the pony's nose. "But I didn't pick a chestnut from the catalogue, Alex."

"No," Alex frowned. "No you didn't, but the ones you picked all went for too much money. I thought she'd be all right. I mean, she's not so bad, is she?"

"Bad?" Kate exclaimed. "Oh Alex, she's a mess. She's so thin, and look at the sores on her back!"

"Oh, come on Kate. She'll be all right." Alex felt embarrassed as everyone seemed to be looking at them.

"How much did she cost?" Kate asked in bewilderment, moving closer to the pony.

"£500," Alex answered.

"£500? Oh Alex, that was all of your money and she's in such a state." Kate just stood there, taking it all in. "She's... she's so filthy and... and..."

Alex saw tears of pity well up in Kate's eyes and for the first time that day he realized the situation was actually pretty bad.

"She's not even registering me," Kate said,

cradling the pony's head in her arms. "It's as though she's given up on life."

"Look," Alex interrupted her firmly. "We can't sit here all day and talk about how bad she looks. We need to move on from here."

"Yes, I guess you're right," Kate said. "Although Nick's not going to be very happy. He's expecting a fit, healthy horse."

"I suppose," Alex faltered and turned away.

"Alex?" Kate grabbed her brother's arm and tried to twist him back. "You have spoken to Nick, haven't you?"

Alex didn't say anything and, as Kate watched him, a look of disbelief crossed her face. "Uh oh, you haven't spoken to him, have you? You never told him you were going to buy Sandy Lane a pony."

"Well, there wasn't really time and anyway, I'm sort of doing him a favour, aren't I? He's bound to be pleased."

Kate looked shocked. "You should still have asked his permission. What if he said he didn't want another pony? I can't believe it – there I was thinking Nick didn't mention it this afternoon because he was too busy. Well, I hope Nick's in a good mood."

"Look Kate." Alex was short. "You're just worrying unnecessarily. Everything will be all right when we get there. She just needs feeding up and grooming, doesn't she?"

"Well, if you say so." But Kate looked doubtful.

"So can you lend me a tenner?" Alex started.

"Ten pounds? What for?" Kate looked really

exasperated now.

"For the box ride back," Alex said.

"You mean you've just gone and spent £500 on a pony and you can't even afford to pay her transport?"

Alex shrugged noncommittally. "I've got a fiver, but it's £15 to Sandy Lane."

"All right, all right," Kate sighed, turning out her pockets. "I've got about £10 in change – it's the money from that sponsored ride I did last week for the Rook Hospital for injured horses. You can borrow it, but I'll need it back tomorrow."

"Of course. That's great," Alex said.

"I don't know how you dare sound so confident," Kate said crossly. "You go and sort out a box driver to take her and I'll try and get the worst of this dirt off her coat." And with that, Kate took a body brush to the little pony's back.

*

It didn't take Alex long to find a box driver going in the direction of Sandy Lane and soon they were on their way. It wasn't a long drive, but Alex was pretty quiet. He was pretty sure that Kate was worrying unnecessarily.

As the box drew to a halt in the yard, Alex looked out of the side window. The yard was pretty busy with riders, madly grooming and tacking up for the afternoon's rides. Calmly, Alex got out of the cab, looking around him as Kate slid out the other side. There was Nick now – coming out of the tack room with his wife, Sarah, at his side, carrying their baby, Zoe.

"Hello Alex. What's with the horsebox?" Nick called across.

In no time at all, the rest of the Sandy Lane riders had gathered around, asking questions.

"Oh hi, Nick. You'll see in a moment," Alex answered.

As the box driver slid down the ramp, the faces of six horses and ponies peered out.

"There, there," Alex mumbled as he stepped up into the box and led the little chestnut pony down the ramp.

"I'm off then," the box driver said.

"OK," Alex said. "And thanks again."

The box driver drove out of the yard, leaving Alex standing there, holding onto the leadrope of the forlorn pony.

"Who does this pony belong to?" Nick looked bemused.

"Well... um, I guess you could say she's mine." Alex tried to look calm – as though turning up at Sandy Lane with a pony in tow was an everyday event. "Actually, I... er... bought her for you."

"For us?" Nick looked shocked. "What do you mean?"

"Well, you know the other night when I was here?" Alex patted the pony's neck.

28

"Yes," Nick wrinkled up his brow.

"Well, you were saying you needed more mounts for Sandy Lane," Alex looked from Nick to Sarah. "So I thought I'd get you one to use for the summer."

"You thought you'd get us a pony and you didn't even ask us if we wanted one?"

"Um, well, there wasn't really time." Alex looked a little embarrassed as he twisted the end of the pony's rope in his hands.

Nick raised his eyebrows. "Kate..." he turned to Alex's sister. "Did you have a hand in this?"

"No, I mean, well..." Kate blustered. "I knew Alex was going to do it." She looked embarrassed. "But I thought he'd talk to you first."

"Have you taken a proper look at this pony?" Nick said, looking her up and down. "She's in a terrible state."

Alex intervened. "Well, I know she's a bit grubby and she's a little on the thin side..."

"A little on the thin side?" Nick exploded. "I'd say that was a bit of an understatement. Where did you get her from?"

"The Ash Hill Sale," Alex admitted. "I thought I'd get something a bit better-looking for my money but..."

"This isn't a toy we're talking about, Alex," Nick interrupted. "What on earth did you think you were doing? What's this all about?"

"Well, I guess it's an investment," Alex said. "I thought I'd let you use her, then sell her on at the end of the summer – maybe make a bit of a profit."

Nick rolled his eyes in disbelief. "I might have known it. Well, we don't need any more ponies – especially one that clearly isn't well. Our friend, Dick Bryant, has agreed to lend us more mounts. We've got three arriving on Monday so you'll have to find somewhere else for her. I'm not being mean but we simply haven't got the room for another pony. Now, if you don't mind, I've got a lesson to take."

And with that, Nick walked off in the direction of the tack room.

"But... but..." Alex was flabbergasted. He stood, holding the pony, and turned to Sarah. "What am I going to do with her, Sarah? I mean, I haven't got anywhere else to keep her."

"You heard what Nick said." Sarah looked embarrassed. "I mean, what did your parents say about it?"

"My parents? Well, I haven't told them yet," Alex said quickly.

"You haven't told them?" Sarah exclaimed.

"But you said..." Kate began.

"Well, I didn't get round to it," Alex said.

"So where did you get the money?" Sarah asked.

"From a premium bond I won. It was mine, don't worry."

"Even so, I think you should have told them," Sarah said. "What are you going to do now? I mean, where are you going to keep this poor pony?"

"I don't know." Alex's voice was a low grunt.

"Oh good grief," Sarah sighed. "Look, I'll have a word with Nick and see if I can sort something out, just for the time being." And with that, Sarah made her way into the tack room.

As Sarah disappeared, Alex turned to his sister. "What am I going to do if I can't keep her here?"

"I'm afraid that's your problem, Alex," Kate fumed. "Thanks to you it looks like I've had a hand in all this. What on earth is Nick going to think of me? And just after he's given up his time to give me extra training with Feather too."

"Oh shut up, Kate," Alex snapped. "I've got enough on my plate without having to worry about what Nick thinks of you."

*

It was only a few minutes later that Nick and Sarah emerged from the tack room. Alex had taken the pony over to a patch of grass and she stood, quietly grazing, as Nick approached.

"I guess we'd better try and talk this through, Alex," Nick started slowly. "Sarah's explained that you haven't got anywhere to keep this pony, but the fact remains that we don't really need her either – especially as we clearly can't use her in lessons."

"I just didn't think this all through," Alex admitted.

"Too right you didn't," Nick said, looking critically at the pony.

Alex waited for Nick to go on.

"As far as I can see, you've got two options," Nick

hesitated. "You can either give this pony to a horse sanctuary or..." At this point Nick took a deep breath. "I'll let you keep her here for the summer if – and only if – you take full responsibility for her. She's not well enough to go outside in the fields, so she'll have to use Whispering Silver's box. Whisp will be all right outside for a few weeks. This pony's going to need extra care, so you'll have to be here every morning to muck her out and groom her, prepare all her foods... really look after her like she's your own pony. I mean she *is* your own pony."

"Every day?" Alex gulped.

"That's what I said." Nick was serious. "Who else do you think is going to do it? It'll be up to you to get her well. She isn't anyone else's responsibility."

"But I won't be able to be here every day," Alex said. "You see, I've got cricket practices three mornings a week and–"

"That's my offer." Nick cut him off short. "Take it or leave it."

Alex was silent. He couldn't think what to say.

"I'm not saying you can't go to your cricket practices," Nick said quickly. "Only that you'll have to fit them around looking after this pony if you want her to stay here. If you get your jobs done in good time, what you do afterwards is your own business."

Alex looked from Nick to the pony. It was the best offer he was going to get. There wasn't a lot else he could do. As much as Alex hated the thought of spending his time looking after a pony, the thought of losing all of his savings was even worse.

"Yes, well OK, I'll do it. I'll take care of her," Alex answered resentfully.

"Good. I expect you to stand by your decision," Nick said firmly. "And I don't want you going to Kate for help. She's going to have her work cut out this summer training Feather for the shows."

"Yes, I know," Alex said.

"And one more thing – you must tell your parents what you've done."

"OK," Alex said slowly.

"Right, well if that's all decided, we'd better get her stabled." Quickly Nick ran a hand down the pony's legs. "She's sound, which is the main thing, and she's got nice lines even if she is very thin. The dirt's pretty thick on that shaggy winter coat, but you'll get it off with cleaning. Take her over to the end box and make her a bran mash. There are worming sachets in the medicine cabinet in the tack room. What's she called by the way?"

In all the excitement of the goings-on in the afternoon, no one had even thought to ask about a name – not even Kate. Alex racked his brains.

"Puzzle." The word came out automatically.

"What?" Nick looked astounded.

"Puzzle – that's what it said in the catalogue," Alex muttered under his breath.

"Well, Puzzle it is then," Nick said. "Unless you want to change it?"

"No, Puzzle's fine," Alex said firmly, leading the pony across the yard. As he pulled back the bolt of Whispering Silver's empty stable, he took a deep breath and led Puzzle inside. Tying her to a ring in the wall, he hurried off to the feed room. Kate was already there ahead of him, mixing up the bran mash.

"Don't think I'll do this every time." She raised her eyebrows. "But Mum and Dad'll be expecting us home soon – and you've got a lot of explaining to do."

"I know, but listen Kate, I'm not going to tell them just yet," Alex said, taking over the stirring. "Maybe in a day or two, but not right now. So don't go saying anything, will you? I want to give her a chance to get on the road to recovery before they know."

"But... but," Kate started, stopping when Alex turned to glare at her. "Well, if you think that's for the best," she finished.

"I do," Alex said, turning his back on Kate. The last thing he wanted at this stage was his parents getting involved. He knew they'd be furious. Right now he needed to put all his energy into getting this wretched pony better – or he'd never see his money again.

5

ONE VERY SICK PONY

Alex joined Kate in the kitchen early the next morning. His mother looked surprised to see him in jodhpurs and riding boots on a Sunday.

"Haven't you got a cricket match today?" she said.

"Yes, yes of course I have, but later," he said, quickly turning away.

Alex grabbed his riding hat and joined Kate at the door. His cricket wasn't until 12 o'clock so if he hurried through his jobs at the yard, he should still be able to make it in time. He was silent as Kate called goodbye for the two of them and they walked out of the house.

"All right, grumpy?" Kate called as Alex unchained his bike.

"Not really," he grunted as they swung their bikes out of the drive and set off down the road. "I can't believe I've got to go to the stables on a Sunday morning!"

"Well, you're the one who bought the pony," Kate said in an exasperated voice. "No one forced you. I don't know – you haven't even started looking after Puzzle yet and already you're grumbling."

"Nobody said I had to smile while I was doing it, did they?" Alex said furiously. "This whole thing's a nightmare. I mean – if I don't get Puzzle well I won't have any money at all, and that will be the end of the cricket tour for sure."

"Yup," Kate answered him.

Alex said nothing as they cycled along. He pedalled hard, silently fuming and trying to resign himself to the morning ahead. In no time at all they reached the bottom of the drive that led to the stables. They turned off the road and headed up past the outdoor school. A muddy Land Rover passed them on the way.

"Isn't that the vet's Land Rover?" Kate looked surprised.

"Looks like it," Alex said. "I guess he's come to look at the lame ponies."

"Yeah, you're probably right. I hope they haven't made their injuries worse," Kate said, wobbling about as she steered through the pot-holes and drew to a halt in the yard.

The stables was already busy that morning. Nick and Sarah were over by the corner stable and there were three or four people crowded around them. But what struck Alex most was the noise. Horses and ponies were whinnying loudly, and the sound of crashing hooves on timber echoed around the yard. Before Alex and Kate even had a chance to go over, Tom had walked across the yard towards them.

"I wouldn't like to be in your shoes right now, Alex," he said.

"What's going on?" Kate asked in a frightened voice.

"It's that pony you brought here," Tom answered. "She's been trying to kick the box down for hours. Nick's been up since six trying to calm her."

"What!" Alex looked shocked. "But she was as quiet as a mouse yesterday."

Tom shrugged his shoulders. "Seems she was probably on tranquillisers at the sale."

Alex swallowed hard. That would be all he needed. Grimly, he mustered up the courage to cross the yard. Nick was already ushering the other people away as Alex reached him.

"What's wrong with her?" Alex asked straight out.

"I don't really know. The vet's with her now," Nick muttered grimly, walking into the box. "He's trying to calm her down."

Alex looked into the box, not daring to say a word. Puzzle stood inside, the whites of her eyes flashing angrily. There was no way he was going in with her.

"So where did you say you got this pony from?" the vet called over his shoulder.

"Alex bought her at the Ash Hill Sale," Nick nodded in Alex's direction.

"Ah," the vet answered. "Well, I've given her a shot to keep her quiet."

"What are the chances of keeping her calm when that wears off?" Nick asked.

"Hard to tell." The vet shrugged. "She's pretty scared, but that's understandable – new home and all that. Whoever her previous owners were, they haven't been treating her very well, have they? She's so thin, and they must have been riding her in pretty uncomfortable tack to make those saddle sores. It's no wonder she flinches when anyone goes near her. Even if you manage to keep her calm, she needs a lot of feeding up. It doesn't even look as though she's touched that haynet either."

"No, she hasn't," Nick admitted. "And she didn't want any of the bran mash we made for her yesterday either."

"It really depends on how well she responds as to whether you'll be able to pull her through. I know you managed it with Storm Cloud, but this pony's in a much worse state."

"But with proper care and attention it should be possible, shouldn't it?" Nick looked concerned.

The vet shrugged. "Only time will tell. I'll leave you with enough tranquilliser to get her through the worst. If she doesn't settle in the next day or so, call me back. If she doesn't improve, you should think about putting her down."

Nick looked thoughtful. "Have you got all of that Alex?"

"I think so," Alex answered. He was shell-shocked. He hadn't imagined for one moment that the pony was so bad that she might have to be put down.

"It doesn't look good," Nick started. "Let's just hope she settles. We can't keep her doped up all summer, and it wouldn't be fair to try and sell her on, or even give her away for that matter. She could cause someone to have a serious accident."

Alex didn't know what to say.

"OK," the vet finished. "I've got to get to Grange Farm now – some problem with their bullocks. Someone needs to stay with her this afternoon – just in case she freaks out again, and I'll leave you with an ointment for those sores."

"Thanks for coming over so promptly," Nick said, following the vet out of the stable.

As they walked over to the Land Rover, Alex turned to Kate, looking embarrassed.

"Did you hear all that?" Alex took a deep breath. "As if things aren't bad enough already. Not only is the pony sick, she's crazy as well!"

*

Alex was relieved that nobody asked him what his parents had said about the pony. With everything that had happened that morning, it must have slipped their minds. Alex kept well out of sight and set about looking after Puzzle. As he pulled back the bolt to her stable, he actually felt pretty nervous, having seen what she was capable of. What if she had another freak-out? Tentatively, Alex approached the pony, but

39

she didn't even move. It looked as if she was still calm from the effects of the tranquilliser, which put Alex's mind at rest. As he groomed her and picked out her hooves, he didn't have too much of a problem. She didn't even bat an eyelid as he bathed her sores and put the ointment on them.

Now, as Alex headed off across the yard to prepare her a bran mash, his heart sank. As he stirred the mixture in the feed room, he thought about the afternoon ahead of him. The vet had said someone needed to stay with Puzzle, and he knew that someone would have to be him. He wouldn't be able to go to cricket as he'd planned. Alex rolled his eyes. Suddenly he was aware of a voice calling into the feed room.

"Hi there."

Alex turned round and looked over the door. There was Izzy standing in front of him.

"Izzy!" He forced a smile to his face. "How are you doing?"

"Looking forward to the summer," Izzy smiled. "How about you? I hear you're going to be spending a bit more time at Sandy Lane now."

"I guess you could say that," Alex grumbled, feeling irritated that the gossip had already spread. "I feel like I've been running around here for hours already."

"Oh, it's not that bad, is it?" Izzy tucked a strand of hair behind her ear.

"Well, you know," Alex tried to look nonchalant as he stood taking another look at Izzy. She'd changed a lot in the year she'd been away at school. Alex hadn't taken much notice of her before. Now, however, he saw that her once long, tangly brown hair was cut short to shoulder length, and he'd forgotten just how green her eyes were. For some reason he suddenly felt tongue-tied.

"Alex, are you listening to me?"

"Yes, yes of course I am," Alex answered.

"I was saying that Kate told me all about Puzzle, and I think it's brilliant of you."

"Brilliant?" Alex relaxed. At least Kate hadn't made him look a complete fool.

"Well there's a bit more to it than that..." He was about to elaborate, but then he stopped. He wouldn't be painting himself in a very good light if he told her he was more worried about getting his money back.

"So are you coming out on the beach hack?" Izzy asked.

"Don't think so, I've got to stay here with Puzzle," Alex answered. "Are you?"

"Course I am, I wouldn't miss it for the world. I guess I'll see you later then," Izzy laughed, catching his eye and disappearing off. Alex stood in the doorway, watching her cross the yard. As she untied Midnight and sprang up into his saddle, Alex was left, holding the bucket of bran mash in his hands, feeling a bit odd.

He looked down at the pail. He ought to take it to Puzzle. Slowly, Alex walked over to Puzzle's stable and looked inside. It was dark in the stable after the bright sunshine of the yard but as Alex's eyes adjusted to the gloom, he could see the pony quite clearly.

Puzzle lifted her head at his approach, and looked warily at him as he pulled back the bolt and placed the bucket of bran mash on the floor.

He didn't wait to watch her eat, but shut the door, leaning back on it as he looked out across the yard. It had filled up while he'd been talking to Izzy. Riders were spilling out of each of the stables with their ponies. And then Alex felt a sharp nip on his wrist.

"Hey." Alex turned round and saw Puzzle standing behind him. That had hurt and he felt angry. "What did you do that for?" His raised words startled the pony and she laid her ears back. "What do you think you're playing at?" Alex looked down at his wrist. The bite hadn't drawn blood, but the teeth marks were pretty clear.

"Miserable thing," Alex muttered. And without another glance, he shot off across the yard.

"What's up with you?" Kate called over.

"Nothing," Alex grumbled. "Just that rotten pony – she's taken a lump out of my wrist."

"Let's see," Kate said, walking over and trying to stifle a giggle.

"It's not funny," he said, showing her his arm.

"Oh Alex." And now Kate burst out laughing. "There's hardly a mark there. You've got to be patient with her. It's hardly surprising she's given you a nip when you consider how badly she's been treated in the past. You've got to try and win her trust back."

"I can't be dealing with all of that," Alex grunted. "Anyway, I've got to go and make a phone call. It looks like I won't be making the cricket this afternoon so I'd better let them know. What a summer!"

"Well, you might not have to spend all of the summer at Sandy Lane if the vet turns out to be right anyway." Kate raised her eyebrows.

"What do you mean?" Alex answered.

"Well, if she doesn't stay calm, Nick said she might have to be put down, didn't he?"

"Not on your life," Alex said fiercely. "I'm going to make sure she stays calm. There's no way I'm having her put down – that would mean I'd lose my £500."

"I'm glad to hear it." Kate raised her eyebrows.

But Alex was already striding off to the feed room so he didn't hear Kate's words. Kate smiled to herself. It might not be for the right reasons, but she'd made her brother more determined than ever to get the pony fit and healthy – exactly the effect she'd intended. Not bad for a little sister.

6

TIRESOME DAYS!

The next couple of days at Sandy Lane were hard work for Alex. Puzzle didn't have any more freak-outs, but Alex still found himself spending most of the day with her. At least she was eating now which was a start. But while she seemed to be holding her own, Alex was missing cricket practice.

On Monday, the replacement ponies arrived, causing great excitement in the yard, and Alex was pleased that everyone's attention was deflected away from his pony. Nick had set up a programme of showjumping practices in the outdoor school and everyone was busy trying them out.

As Alex cycled to the stables on Wednesday morning, he gritted his teeth. He was late. He counted off the list of chores in his head – soaping Puzzle's mane and tail, washing her coat, picking out her hooves, putting the ointment on her saddle sores... and that was just the start. He'd still have to groom her again in the afternoon *and* lead her around the yard. Nick had said she wasn't ready to go out into the fields, but she still needed the exercise. Around and around the yard – it was so boring. Alex's mind was so far away, that he didn't even notice Jess freewheeling into Sandy Lane at the same time as him.

"Look out!" Jess cried as she swerved to avoid a collision.

"Sorry," Alex called, following her up the drive and into the yard. Most of the horses and ponies were out of their stables and basking in the summer sun as Alex jumped off his bike and propped it up against the barn. He headed across the yard for Puzzle's stable and tentatively slid back the bolt. The chestnut pony backed away into the corner of the stable as he walked inside, her ears flat back.

"Wretched thing," Alex grunted.

But he wasn't scared of her as he had been that first day, and didn't falter as he picked up a body brush and set to work on her coat. As he finished picking out her hooves and wiping down her coat, he let himself out of her stable and made his way to get her food. Depositing a haynet with the little pony, he left her eating as he walked over to the hay bales. The sky was a deep blue, and there wasn't a cloud in sight as he lay back. Maybe – just maybe, he'd be able to make the cricket practice this afternoon.

Alex sat up and looked around the yard. He could

see the back of Tom's head in Chancey's stable. Rosie and Jess were grooming Pepper and Skylark while Izzy was leading Midnight into the yard. They were all so keen. Alex flopped back on the bales.

"Hey Alex, how are you getting on?" Alex heard his sister's voice, and sat up.

"All right I guess. I've cleaned her, but I've still got to walk her around this afternoon. I'll have to miss cricket practice again."

"Oh well, I guess the most important thing now is getting Puzzle well again," Kate said.

"At this very moment, I couldn't care less if I never see her again," Alex snapped.

"Oh Alex." Kate looked cross. "You could be a little bit kinder to her. Remember she's been through a lot. The odd pat or kind word wouldn't go amiss. Ponies need love and attention too, you know." Kate's voice wobbled a bit as she said this.

"You know I'm not into all that," Alex groaned. "Look, I don't suppose you'd do me a favour, would you?"

"What?" Kate looked warily at him.

"It's not a lot – just put the ointment on Puzzle's sores and walk her around the yard this afternoon. It would mean I could leave now to get to cricket," Alex wheedled.

"Oh Alex, I would do it, but I'm supposed to be training Feather this afternoon," Kate groaned.

"Just this once, Kate. My chances of staying in the squad aren't good if I don't make the practice. It's really important."

"I don't know," Kate hesitated.

"Oh forget it." Alex turned back to glare at Puzzle. "I might have known you wouldn't help me out. Just remember that the next time you want a favour!"

"Oh Alex," Kate sighed. "All right, I'll do it."

"Brilliant!" Alex's face brightened.

"Remember I'm only doing it for Puzzle," Kate said crossly. "I don't mind helping you out with her this once, but I'll be pretty busy with Feather and the shows after that."

"I know. Thanks Kate!" Alex jumped to his feet before she could change her mind. Grinning, he made off across the yard. "I'll make it up to you," he called back over his shoulder. "You won't regret this."

Kate shook her head, watching as her brother rushed off out of the yard, and then she turned round and looked back over to Puzzle's stable. The little chestnut pony hung her head over her stable door and Kate felt a pang of guilt as she saw her. Alex might be looking after her all right, but at this moment, all that Puzzle really needed was a friend. Sadly Kate walked over to the little pony and held out her hand.

"There there," she said, patting Puzzle's neck. "He didn't really mean all those things he said about you."

*

"You're very quiet, Alex. Is something bothering you?" his mother asked at the breakfast table on Sunday morning.

"Not really," Alex answered.

"What time does your cricket match start?" Mr. Hardy looked up from his paper. "I thought I might come along and watch."

"Actually, I'm not playing today." Alex spooned the cereal around in his bowl. "I've been dropped from the squad." It was the first time he'd told anyone what had happened when he'd gone to the cricket practice on Wednesday afternoon. His place on the school tour was still certain but he was annoyed at being dropped from the squad. He'd been trying not to think about it though. He'd got to the practice on time all right, but that didn't alter the fact that he'd missed so many other practices. His cricket coach hadn't been very understanding about it.

Mr. Hardy put down his newspaper, looking taken aback. "So what's happened, Alex?"

"Well, the coach has given my place to someone else," Alex said miserably.

"Oh Alex," his mother joined in. "What a shame."

The last thing Alex needed was his mother rubbing salt into the wound.

"I'll get my place back, it's no big deal." Alex gritted his teeth. "Come on, we're going to be late, Kate."

"Where are you off to now?" his mother asked.

"Sandy Lane," Alex answered gruffly.

"The stables?" his mother looked surprised. "Well,

48

it's no wonder you've been dropped, the amount of time you spend down there. If you've made a commitment to a team, you should keep it, you know."

"Have you been missing practices, Alex?" Mr. Hardy looked up from his paper.

"Look it's nothing Dad." Alex was fuming as he headed for the door. It was bad enough having missed cricket to be at Sandy Lane, but being reprimanded for it too...

"Wait a minute, Alex, I'm coming," Kate called.

Alex left the front door open behind him and hurried over to his bike. As he sat in the saddle, feet on the ground, he waited for Kate to join him. Finally, the front door slammed shut and she made her way over to him.

"I know you're fed up about this cricket business," she said. "But getting angry isn't going to help."

"Isn't it?" Alex grunted. "But I *am* angry."

"Look," Kate shrugged. "Now that you've got more time to spend at Sandy Lane, why don't you make the most of it and come to some of the jumping practices too? You'll still be there to look after Puzzle and it'll be a break from running around her all the time. You never know, you might even enjoy it."

"Doubt it," Alex grunted, pedalling away.

"Oh well, it's up to you," Kate cried, racing up behind him, and speeding on.

As Alex's bike bumped over the pot-holes, he thought about what Kate had said. Maybe it would make things easier if he went for a ride – at least it would make a change from mucking out and grooming. As he cycled into the yard, Rosie and Jess called across to him.

"Hi Alex."

"Hi," Alex grunted, drawing to a halt as Tom walked over to him.

"We're jumping in half an hour. You coming?" he said.

"Dunno," Alex replied.

"Come on," Tom pushed him. "You could ride Hector. Why don't I go and check he's not booked. I'm sure Nick won't mind." And before Alex could say anything to stop him, Tom was disappearing in the direction of the tack room.

"It seems my mind's been made up for me." Alex turned to where Rosie and Jess were standing. Then Tom appeared at the doorway of the tack room.

"No one's riding Hector, so you're up," he said. "Nick's all agreed so there's no bottling out."

"All right, all right," Alex grinned. "I'd better go and sort out Puzzle first then." He rushed off across the yard, leaving Tom behind him.

Drawing back the bolt to Puzzle's stable, Alex stepped inside. Puzzle didn't bat an eyelid this morning as Alex picked up the body brush and began to sweep the brush over her back. There was just enough time for her ointment, then he'd have to go and get Hector ready. He stood back and looked at the little chestnut pony. She was still thin, but at least her coat was clean and starting to shine again. Alex tried not to look too closely at the sores on her back. They still made him feel a bit ill.

"There, all done." Alex drew back the bolt and stepped outside. He took one quick look back, then he made his way across the yard and tacked up Hector. As he led the large gelding out of his stable, the warm summer sun bore down on Alex's back. It was baking out in the yard.

As Nick appeared, the horses and riders made their way down the drive to the outdoor school. Kate was there on Feather, and then there was Tom with Chancey. Alex looked back over his shoulder to see Rosie and Jess mount up on Jester and Skylark and now Izzy came trotting past on Midnight.

"Hello Alex," she smiled.

"Oh hi Izzy." Alex hadn't seen her for the last couple of days and he felt pleased. It was a long time since Alex had gone to a jumping practice, so he hoped he wouldn't show himself up in front of her. He came to a halt in the middle of the school and listened hard to what Nick was saying.

"As you can see." Nick's voice boomed out. "It's a simple figure-of-eight course. Nothing too hard, so concentrate on your rhythm and poise. Tom, why don't you lead off and show us how it's done."

Alex watched with interest as Tom cantered a circle and approached the first jump. He'd ridden with his friend loads of times in the past but he hadn't seen Chancey and Tom jump together for a while. As they cleared the brush, Alex was pretty impressed. They'd really come on. Tom had the chestnut gelding well in hand and they jumped with ease. It was obvious they were a perfect team as they soared over the gate and cantered a turn for the staircase. Effortlessly, they soared over the jump as if it wasn't there and approached the triple bars in a collected canter. Tom rode Chancey at the middle of the jump and Chancey responded to Tom's command. They cleared the jump, landing lightly to turn for the parallel. Over that... and now there was just the treble. As they cleared the last jump, Tom drew Chancey to a halt by the group.

"Pretty good, Tom," Nick called. "You lost your position a bit at the stile, but apart from that – not bad."

Alex looked amazed. It had looked perfect to him. What would Nick have to say about his riding? But there wasn't time to dwell on it as Kate was called. Alex turned his attention to his sister. Fluidly Kate and Feather jumped each of the jumps, clearing the course in easy strides. Alex wasn't surprised – they'd been practising pretty hard lately. He started to feel apprehensive. What if he was the only one to show himself up? Patiently he sat, waiting for his name to be called and then Jess went forward.

Skylark was pulling like a steam train as they approached the brush jump and narrowly missed knocking the whole lot over, but at least they were clear and now they were onto the next. Alex could see that Jess was having difficulty holding the horse. Jess's face was pale with concentration as she positioned Skylark at the staircase. Skylark leaned back on her hocks and sprang forward for the jump. It stayed up, though Alex didn't know how. As they rode at the triple bars, they weren't going to be so lucky. Skylark cruised towards the jump at high speed and there was nothing Jess could do to stop her from clipping the top. A pole clattered down behind her. Alex grimaced and now that Skylark was sweated up, he could see Jess was going to have problems with the last two jumps. Sure enough, she clattered her way through the parallel and knocked down the treble.

"Don't worry too much about that, Jess," Nick called. "She's obviously having an off-day."

When Alex's name was called, he already felt a bit apprehensive.

"Concentrate... concentrate," he muttered to himself, cantering Hector to the first. He was so anxious that he checked his horse in the take-off. Hector hesitated and heaved himself forward, leaving Alex hanging in mid-air. Alex landed in a pile on Hector's neck. He gritted his teeth and picked himself up before cantering to the gate. This time he let Hector have his head and they cleared it without hesitation. Alex started to relax as they cantered to the staircase. Everything that he'd learned started to come back to him and the next two jumps weren't too much of a problem. As Alex cleared the triple bars, he returned to the group, feeling quietly pleased.

"Not bad at all," Nick called.

Alex grinned. He'd rather enjoyed that. He watched as Izzy and Rosie rode the course, and wished he could have another go.

"That's all for today," said Nick. "We've been out here for half an hour now. There's a hack going out at

11 o'clock, so I think we'll take the horses back. I don't want them to get too tired."

Slowly the riders started to make their way back to the yard.

"Alex, hang on a minute," Nick called. "I've got something for you. I'm afraid it's the vet's bill for Puzzle. Can I leave you to settle it, or would you like me to do it? You can pay me when you've spoken to your parents, if you like."

Alex gulped. "I don't know. Er... how much is it?"

"£50," Nick answered.

"Would you mind settling it for me, Nick?" Alex said quickly, feeling embarrassed. "I could give it to you later this week."

"That's fine," Nick said, opening the gate.

As they walked side by side up the drive, Nick changed the subject to the approaching Benbridge Show. Alex nodded as Nick spoke, but his mind wasn't with it at all. Where on earth was he going to get £50 from? He couldn't go to his parents for help, could he?

Alex felt his face flush as he parted ways with Nick. Quickly he led Hector to his stable and started to untack him and rub him down. What could he do? Who could he go to? There was only one person he could ask for that money... only one person who knew the situation he was in.

Alex closed the door on Hector and made his way over to where Kate was grooming Feather.

"Hi there," he said, trying to look nonchalant.

"What do you want?" Kate said, able to read her

54

brother like a book.

"Puzzle's bill from the vet has come in." Alex cut straight to the point. "And Nick expects me to pay it."

"And?" Kate didn't look surprised.

"*And* I don't have the money," Alex said exasperatedly. "I was hoping you might be able to lend it to me."

"No way." Kate looked fed-up. "You still haven't given me back the £10 you borrowed at the sale."

"I know... I know, but I will," Alex pleaded. "Come on, there isn't anyone else I can ask, and it is for Puzzle."

"How much is it?" Kate said guardedly.

"£50."

"£50!" Kate gasped. "But... I mean, that's such a lot. How am I going to find £50?"

"Look, I know that you've got it in your savings account," Alex wheedled.

"Yes, but I need that," Kate said. "Mum and Dad said I can only go skiing at Christmas if I contribute. The deposit's due at the beginning of term."

"But I'd pay you back before then," Alex said.

"How?" Kate said warily. "Given your track record with money it's unlikely I'll see the money again."

"That's not fair." Alex was starting to feel hassled now.

Kate looked thoughtful. "All right, Alex," she said, "I'll lend it to you, but only if you swear you'll give it back to me before we go back to school."

"I swear," Alex said solemnly as Kate walked out

of Feather's stable and off across the yard. Alex stared after her. Just as he'd thought things were picking up. Was there no end to the problems that Puzzle was going to throw up?

7

TURNING POINT

As Alex turned up the driveway to the stables a week later, he felt tired and fed-up. He propped his bike up by the barn and started to walk across the yard. Before he even had a chance to get to Puzzle's stable, she lifted her head over her stable door, and whinnied loudly.

Alex stood quite still. He looked around him to see who she was calling to, but the yard was empty. As he made his way over to her, she whinnied again. Tentatively Alex drew back the door and held out a peppermint for her.

"All right in there?" he grunted begrudgingly. Alex laid a hand on her nose and spoke in a quiet voice as he patted her neck. "Come on then."

Puzzle sniffed at the offering. But just at that

moment, a loud voice came from behind him...

"Hey there!" And Puzzle's head shot back up.

Alex looked out over the box to see Tom striding over towards him.

"Are you coming to the jumping practice again today?" Tom asked cheerily.

"Nah – don't think I'll bother," Alex said, stepping out of Puzzle's box and bolting the door.

"Why not? You did pretty well last time," Tom said.

"Oh, I don't know." Alex looked behind him and saw that the yard was filling up – all the regular riders were gathering with their mounts. And if he wasn't mistaken, Charlie Marshall was striding up the drive too.

Charlie used to be a regular rider at Sandy Lane, but he'd started at racing school last September, and it wasn't often that he found the time to get back to see them. Alex was pleased to see him.

"Charlie," he called over. "How are you doing?"

"Great, just great," Charlie answered, walking over to Tom and Alex and clapping them on the back.

"What are you doing here?" Tom asked. "Bored of the racehorses already?"

"Oh you know – I just thought I'd call in and see what the amateurs were up to," Charlie swaggered.

Tom gave him a joking thump on the back.

"No, actually, I'm home for the weekend," Charlie went on. "So I gave Nick a ring to see if I could book a ride with my old Sandy Lane mates, only it appears you're all practising for the Benbridge Show. I thought

I'd come along and show you how it's done."

"Ha ha, I suppose that's meant to be a joke," Tom laughed.

"No, I'm being perfectly serious," Charlie grinned.

"Well, I'm afraid I'm not going to be joining you," Alex joined in. "I've got to get Puzzle some vitamin supplements from the fodder merchant's."

"Puzzle? Who's Puzzle?" Charlie butted in. "Is there a new pony at the yard?" Suddenly he looked interested as he leaned into the box beside him. "Oh yikes." He turned his nose up disdainfully. "Where did that mangy old thing come from?"

Alex looked into the box. He'd thought Puzzle had been looking a lot better lately, but after what Charlie had said, he didn't want to admit that she was his pony.

"You should have seen her a few weeks ago," Alex said. "She was so thin back then. She's started to put on a bit of weight, hasn't she Tom?"

"She certainly has," Tom answered.

"Well, if you say so," Charlie shrugged.

"At least she's clean and her saddle sores are healing as well," Tom went on. "She *is* a New Forest pony, Charlie, so she'll never have the sleek, polished coat of one of your thoroughbreds."

"I guess." Charlie shrugged his shoulders. "But put it this way – she's no oil painting, is she? Come on, let's get ready. Nick said I could ride Napoleon. Where's he stabled these days?" And with that, Charlie was striding off across the yard.

Tom turned to Alex. "Look, you're doing a great

job with Puzzle. Don't listen to Charlie. It'll just take time."

Alex nodded and turned away. How much *more* time was he going to have to spend at Sandy Lane before he could get rid of her?

"Are you quite sure you don't want to come to jumping practice?" Tom asked.

"Positive," Alex answered. "I'm fine. You go and tack up Chancey."

"OK," Tom answered, walking away.

Alex looked at Puzzle. Surely she must be on the mend by now after all the work he'd put in. Alex's thoughts were interrupted as Nick walked over.

"How's it going?" he asked.

"Oh, not so bad," Alex shrugged.

"She's been getting bored in her stable." Nick nodded in Puzzle's direction. "It's probably about time we let her out into the fields with the other ponies. She's been looking a bit better so you could try exercising her on a lunge rein."

"Do you think she's ready for that?" Alex looked doubtful. "Charlie thought she was in a terrible state."

"Remember Charlie spends his time with expensive thoroughbreds these days, so take no notice. If Charlie had seen her a few weeks ago he'd have realized there's been a vast improvement, and if you want to be ready to sell her at the end of the summer, she's going to need the exercise."

"Yes, I suppose she is." Alex brightened up at Nick's words. It was the first time he'd made any mention that she might be all right to sell. Perhaps things were looking up. "It's just that I'm not sure how you go about lunging," Alex said. "I've never done it before."

Nick took a deep breath. "I hadn't really planned to get involved with her training, but I might be able to find a little time to help you over the next week. I've got half an hour this afternoon if you want to make a start."

"Really?" Alex breathed a sigh of relief. "So, you don't mind?"

"The more I help you, the quicker I get my stable back!" Nick raised his eyebrows.

"Yes, I guess so," Alex answered.

"So how about we make a start after the jumping practice this afternoon?" Nick said.

"Great," Alex answered.

"OK then," Nick said. "I'll meet you at 3 o'clock." And with that, he walked off down the drive to the outdoor school.

8

A RIDE TO REMEMBER...

It had been just over a week now that Nick and Alex
had been lunging Puzzle – only a little each day, but
she was steadily improving.

As Alex stood in the centre of the field on Sunday
afternoon, he coaxed Puzzle into a canter. Her copper-
coloured coat shone in the sunlight. She was using
Minstrel's saddle which was tied on her back. It looked
funny to see it without any stirrups. As Puzzle cantered
around the school she looked remarkably together.

"She's getting the hang of that," Nick called from
where he was sitting on the rails.

Alex slowed Puzzle down to a trot with the word
"ter-rot".

"Very good." Nick jumped down. "Let's try her
with some loose jumping." He put a couple of low

cross poles up and Alex lunged Puzzle over them.

"You see. She jumps them easily. I was thinking we might try a little weight on her back today," Nick said.

"You mean ride her?" Alex gulped. "Is she ready for that?"

Nick laughed. "Well, I don't see why not. She's going all right on the lunge. She'll get bored if we keep taking her round and round. I'll go and fetch Napoleon so I can ride with you. It'll be good company for her."

"OK," Alex said uncertainly. Lunging Puzzle was one thing, but he wasn't sure he wanted to actually get on her. She hadn't been ridden for ages, and who knew how she might react? Anxiously, Alex bit his bottom lip as Nick appeared again, leading Napoleon over.

"I'll just attach the stirrup irons and leathers to Puzzle's saddle, then we're ready to go," Nick said.

As Alex held the two horses, he wondered how he could back out of this, but now Nick had started talking again.

"Come on... ease yourself gently into the saddle so you don't alarm her." Nick took Napoleon's reins from Alex and sprang up onto the big brown gelding.

Alex felt a bit nervous as he put a leg into the stirrup but Puzzle didn't even flinch, and that gave him the confidence to hop up onto her back. Gently, he settled down into the saddle and gathered up the reins, patting her neck.

"She seems all right, Nick." Alex looked surprised.

A smile spread across Nick's face. "OK, let's ease off at a walk and head for the woods."

Carefully, Alex nudged Puzzle forward through the gate at the back of the outdoor school and into the fields behind. Puzzle didn't hesitate and went forward with ease.

"Shall we try a trot?" Nick suggested.

Alex nodded, squeezing Puzzle on with his legs. She must have been well-trained at some point in her life because she responded without hesitation. Napoleon and Puzzle trotted easily alongside each other.

"All right?" Nick called across.

"I'm just fine," Alex replied. Riding Puzzle actually felt pretty comfortable.

"She looks calm enough," Nick went on. "Let's canter over to the hedge." Nick pointed over to the other side of the field, and now that Alex had got into the swing of things, he started to relax. Gently, he nudged Puzzle forward and they set off into a neat canter. As Nick positioned Napoleon for a fallen tree trunk, Alex didn't even have a chance to think about the size of it. He kicked Puzzle on, coaxing the reins up her neck as he placed her squarely at the trunk. Puzzle flew through the air as if the jump wasn't even there, landing lightly and cantering on into the trees.

"She's done this before," Nick called under his arm. "She cleared it with three feet to spare."

"She did pretty well, didn't she?" Alex answered breathlessly.

"Not bad at all," Nick answered. "Why don't you try her in the jumping practice on Wednesday morning? It'll be good training for her to be around the other horses."

"Yes, all right," Alex answered. Nick was right – she did need to get used to being ridden around other horses. As they walked back to the yard Alex and Nick chattered easily about other things. Alex jumped down off Puzzle's back and led her off to her stable. That ride hadn't been so bad... not bad at all.

Once Alex had rubbed Puzzle down and settled her with a haynet, he went off in search of Kate. It didn't take him long to find her. She was in Feather's stable, wiping a cloth over her coat.

"Are you coming home soon?" he asked her.

"Oh it's you," she laughed. "Yes, I'm just finishing up here." Quickly she closed the door behind the grey pony and walked with Alex to where their bikes were propped up against the old barn.

"You're not going to believe it," Alex said.

"Wow me with it," Kate said tiredly, wheeling her bike into the centre of the yard.

"I rode Puzzle today," Alex told her.

"Really? That's brilliant news." Kate looked surprised. Then she frowned. "But I thought you'd only been lunging her."

"I had been, but Nick thought she was ready for someone on her back." Alex couldn't keep the grin off his face as they set off. "She cleared that tree trunk over by the woods."

"But that's massive." Kate looked amazed.

"Yeah, and I've decided to ride her in the jumping practice on Wednesday morning. Nick thinks it'll be good for her. I don't want to wear her out though..." Alex looked thoughtful.

"Anyone would think you were getting attached to Puzzle, the way you're talking about her." Kate raised her eyebrows.

"Don't talk such rubbish" Alex said gruffly. "You know I'm only doing this because I have to. The sooner I can get her fit and healthy, the sooner I can sell her."

And with that, he pedalled off.

9

JUMPING PRACTICE

There wasn't a cloud in the sky as Alex reached the stables on Wednesday morning. He deposited his bike by the barn and made his way to Puzzle's stable. Drawing back the bolt, he stepped inside. Puzzle looked up from her haynet, but she didn't back away into the corner.

As he patted her neck, she chewed on her hay and went to take a friendly bite out of his jacket. Alex brushed her nose away. "I'll have none of that this morning." But he wasn't angry. He picked up a body brush and set to work on her shaggy coat. He was so engrossed in his work that he didn't even notice that Izzy was at the stable door until she spoke. Alex hadn't bumped into her for a couple of days.

"I hear you and Puzzle are joining us for jumping

practice today," she said. "I can't wait to see what she can do."

"Yeah, well she jumped that log out in the back fields on Sunday," Alex boasted. "So hopefully she should go well in the school too."

"Let's hope so." Izzy tossed back her hair. "I'll catch you later."

"All right." Alex's words tailed off as she turned and walked across the yard. Quickly, he bent down to pick out Puzzle's shoes.

"You'd better not show me up out there today, Puzzle."

"Talking to her now, are you?" It was Kate's head that appeared over the stable door this time, and she grinned as she looked in.

"What?" Alex looked embarrassed. He hadn't realized he was talking aloud.

"Oh nothing," Kate laughed. "Come on. We're off in a moment."

"All right... all right." Alex quickly tacked Puzzle up and led her out into the yard. All of the riders were there – Kate was adjusting Feather's girth, Jess and Rosie were chattering, holding Skylark and Hector, and it looked as though Tom was giving Chancey a little pep talk.

Alex brought Puzzle out to stand alongside Chancey and Feather. The two horses' coats were so polished. Puzzle would never look like them – not even if she was in the best condition. Puzzle's New Forest breeding meant that she was a much hardier, sturdier breed than the part-thoroughbred and Arab.

She could never look as delicate and showy. Alex took a deep breath as Nick appeared and soon they were leading off to the outdoor school and walking into the centre of the ring.

"OK." Nick acted as though there was nothing unusual about Puzzle joining the group. "We're going to start with the brush and go on to the gate," he said, pointing out the direction he wanted the riders to take. "We'll warm the ponies up first. Take your time. I want to see skill and thought put into this. Speed can come at the next practice."

The group set off at a walk around the ring and then Nick called for them to trot. They followed on in single file, till Nick judged it all right for them to canter, one after the other.

"OK, we'll start," Nick called. "Are you ready to lead us off, Jess?"

Jess nodded and turned Skylark to the first jump. Neatly she cantered forward, taking the brush in easy strides. Alex watched as she sat, poised and calm, on the back of her pony. They soared over the gate and Alex felt pleased to see Jess back in control. She must have put in a lot of practice with the pony. As they rode to the staircase, Jess checked Skylark and she just clipped the top of the jump. She was unlucky – the pole came clattering down.

Jess looked under her arm and cantered on to the triple bars, flying over them with ease. Now there were just two jumps left. Skylark swished her tail as they rose for the parallel, landing neatly before going on to the treble. If it hadn't been for that one jump, it would have been a perfect round.

"Good Jess," Nick said.

The sun was beating down on Alex's back as he watched Nick nod to Kate, and waited for his own turn.

As Kate positioned Feather at the brush, Alex gazed into the distance. The sound of cantering hooves filled the air. It wouldn't be long now, but riding a course was quite different to jumping a log out on a hack. Out of the corner of his eye, Alex could see Izzy watching him, and again he was conscious that he wanted to do well.

As Kate pulled Feather up to a halt, Nick waved and called Alex's name.

Alex gave Puzzle a little nudge.

"Easy, easy does it," he muttered under his breath. Alex shut all of the other riders out of his mind as he popped Puzzle over the jump and rode her squarely at the staircase. He collected the pony in the take-off, easing his hands up her neck for the jump and she cleared it with ease. Everything seemed to come naturally once Alex had found a rhythm and Puzzle cantered around the course like an old hand. Alex started to relax as he fed the reins up her neck in the take-off for the triple bars. This was going well...

So well that Alex must have relaxed his concentration a little. Maybe it was because he didn't tell her what he wanted her to do, but Puzzle hesitated in the approach to the triple bars. It looked like she was going to refuse, but at the last minute, she leaned back on her hocks and flung herself forward. But it was too late. She rapped the top of the triple and a bar came down. Alex gritted his teeth, cross at himself for that momentary lapse as he nudged Puzzle forward for the parallel. This time he was back in control and they cleared the fence with inches to spare, touching down effortlessly. Alex turned Puzzle for the treble and, as they cleared the jump, they drew to a halt beside the group.

"Not bad," Nick called.

"That was good, Alex." Kate's eyes gleamed.

"I never imagined she'd be so capable," Izzy agreed.

"If only we hadn't knocked that triple bar," Alex muttered under his breath. He was annoyed with himself.

"You can't expect everything to go perfectly," Nick called over. "You haven't exactly been riding much lately, have you?"

"Well no." Alex knew it had been his fault, but he didn't like it being pointed out in front of everyone. He hated not doing things well.

He hardly watched the rest of the horses complete the course, he was so cross at himself. As the riders made their way back to the yard, all they could talk about was how surprised they were at how well Puzzle had jumped. Alex didn't say anything as he led Puzzle to her stable and started to untack her.

"You didn't ride too badly out there." Nick's smiling face called over the door to him. "You should think about entering the Benbridge Show, you know."

"Oh, I don't know about that." Alex was still feeling

grumpy. "I think Rosie's got her heart set on riding Hector now that Pepper's injured."

"I'm not saying you should ride Hector," Nick laughed. "Ride Puzzle."

"Puzzle?" Alex looked amazed. "I don't know Nick. She's a steady jumper but I'm not sure she could win."

"Win? I'm not saying she could win," Nick frowned.

"Then what's the point of entering," Alex muttered under his breath, looking embarrassed at his mistake.

"Oh Alex," Nick laughed. "You don't enter competitions just to win. She's a solid, sturdy little pony. I'm sure she won't disgrace herself, and it'll be good training for her."

"I guess so." Alex frowned.

"It's up to you," Nick laughed.

Alex nodded. Maybe he should enter Puzzle. Nick was right – it would be good training for her. If he could get her used to competing, it would only make her more saleable. And who knows, maybe she could win? Nick was wrong about competitions, Alex thought to himself. You had to enter them to win – otherwise what was the point of doing them?

10

THE BENBRIDGE SHOW

It didn't take Alex long to make a decision about the Benbridge Show. Once he'd talked to Kate and she'd agreed it was in Puzzle's interest to compete, Alex had decided he'd definitely enter. And for the next week and a half he and Puzzle worked hard – not missing a single jumping practice. It was countdown. The summer days passed quickly and soon there were only three more days before the show... then two... and then Alex was sitting in his bedroom the night before the show.

"All right Alex?" Kate asked, pushing open the door.

"Yeah, I guess," he said.

"What's up? Puzzle's going nicely. You're not having doubts about entering her, are you?" Kate looked concerned.

"No." Alex kicked off his shoes and lay sprawled on the window seat, staring out onto the garden. "It's Mum and Dad. I told them I was riding one of the Sandy Lane ponies at the show. Maybe I ought to tell them what I've done. I was going to tell them once I'd made the money. I don't know... I'll think about it after the show."

"We'd better go down for supper," Kate said. "Mum'll be thinking something's up otherwise."

"OK." Alex put his thoughts to the back of his mind, and climbing off the window seat, made his way down the stairs.

*

The next morning, Alex opened one eye and squinted at the sunlight streaming in through the crack of his curtains. At first he couldn't think what day it was, then he remembered. The Benbridge Show! He checked his watch and leapt out of bed. Dashing to the bathroom, he jumped in and out of the shower and scrambled into his clothes, all in five minutes flat. By the time he got to the kitchen, Kate was already eating breakfast, looking neat and tidy in a pair of cream jodhpurs and navy-blue hacking jacket.

"Why didn't you wake me?" he said breathlessly.

"I'm not your alarm clock." Kate shrugged as he gobbled down a piece of toast. Quickly, Alex picked up his riding hat and threw on the show jacket that Nick had lent him. It was a bit on the large side, but it would have to do.

"Come on then, Kate," he said.

"All right," Kate said indignantly. Mrs. Hardy only just had time to call out 'good luck' as Kate and Alex disappeared out of the door.

It was cool outside – the blistering heat of the last couple of days had passed. Kate and Alex cycled along, talking about the day ahead of them. As they cycled down the driveway to the stables and into the yard, everyone was already rushing around – oiling hooves, searching for grooming kit, plaiting manes and putting studs in hooves. Alex felt a rush of adrenaline flood through him. Without even stopping to talk to anyone, Alex made his way to Puzzle's stable.

"So how are you this morning?" he asked, sliding back the door. "I hope you're feeling on good form."

Meticulously, he ran a body brush over Puzzle's coat and picked out her feet. He combed and plaited her mane and tail and oiled her hooves. He worked hard, until finally he was able to stand back and admire his handiwork. Puzzle was still a little on the thin side, but at least her coat was spotlessly clean. Alex was pleased. He looked at his watch. Eight thirty. If he hurried, he'd be able to join the first group of riders hacking over to the show.

"Bye Kate. I'll see you there," he called over his shoulder to his sister as he joined the pack.

"Bye," Kate answered him.

Four horses set off down the lane, following on one after the other. Alex wasn't paying much attention to what everyone else was saying as they cut across country, making their way through the fallow fields that adjoined Mr. Wells' pig farm. Alex sat, feeling quietly confident. He had a good feeling about today. Rosie was chattering away non-stop, Izzy was looking worried and Tom – well Tom was just quiet.

Soon they broke into an easy canter till they reached a gate to the road. Tom held it open for them to pass through. It wasn't far now. There was another group of riders following along after them with Kate and Jess, and Nick was coming along later with the group of younger riders who were entered for the gymkhana events. When everyone got there, they were to meet under the big oak by the jumping ring.

As Alex rode down the road and turned into the showground, he felt the adrenaline pump through him. He had forgotten what it was like at a show. Entries were being announced over a loudspeaker. Officials were running around. There was a small stand for the judges. It even *smelled* important. Alex felt excited at the thought of the competition ahead of him.

"How many people do you think will enter the Open Jumping, Tom?" Alex asked.

"Maybe 50," Tom said with a shrug.

"50!" Alex hadn't thought it would be as many as that.

"Let's tie up these ponies and take a look," Tom said. Whistling to himself, Alex tied Puzzle to a fence under the shade of the oak tree and followed Tom to the secretary's tent. There, they picked up their numbers. Tom was number 30, and Alex number 42. They tied the numbers onto their backs and then they wandered over to check the jumping order. There were 62 entries in all – even more than Tom had thought.

"Come on, Alex," Tom said. "Let's grab a hot dog."

"Sure thing," Alex grinned. They handed over their money and tucked in. Then they walked past the tents, selling everything from hacking jackets to saddle soap and sweatshirts.

"Beautiful!" Tom pointed to an elegant jet-black horse in the Working Hunter Class.

"Yeah, but come on," Alex said. "We ought to be heading back to the tree – the others will be here by now."

"You're right," Tom said as they hurried back across the showground.

"Where've you been?" Kate's voice was the first to greet him as they reached the tree.

"Just looking around," Alex answered nonchalantly.

"Right, are we ready?" Nick tried to attract everyone's attention. "I want you all to make sure that you limber up your mounts properly before going into your class – the collecting ring is over there." He pointed to the right of him. "Remember that you're here representing Sandy Lane, so I don't want to see anyone fooling around, all right?"

Everyone nodded in agreement.

"Good, well, Sarah will be here any minute. She's

coming in the Land Rover and bringing brushes and stuff for restitching any plaits that are coming loose. Now is there anything else I need to say?" He looked puzzled, as if he had forgotten something, and stood scratching his head. "Oh yes, of course... good luck."

It was the same joke he made at all the shows, but at least it put the riders at their ease.

"Thanks Nick," a medley of voices answered him and soon everyone had disbanded to go their separate ways. Alex didn't know what to do with himself. There was half an hour until the Open Jumping and now he was here, he was so excited, he just wanted to get going. Maybe he'd take a walk. Aimlessly, he wandered past the show classes... past the gymkhana events... until he found he was walking round and round in circles. He ought to go and check on Puzzle. Suddenly he felt really charged up with excitement.

"Are you coming to walk the course?" Rosie and Jess called over to him as he crossed the grass.

"In a moment," Alex answered. He patted Puzzle and made his way over to the ring. Rosie and Jess, and Izzy and Kate, were already there ahead of him. Tom was there too. He looked serious as he stopped by each of the jumps, but then he was under pressure as he'd won this class for the last three years running.

"All right Tom?" Alex walked over and clapped him on the back.

"I don't know, there are some tight corners this year," Tom moaned.

"Oh, we'll be all right." Alex's eyes narrowed as he took the jumps in. And then the loudspeaker was asking them to clear the course. The competition was about to begin.

"Good luck, Alex." Tom said.

"You too, Tom. Good luck Izzy and Kate," he called across the grass.

"Thanks... wait for us." Izzy and Kate joined Alex to make their way back to the group. Alex untied Puzzle and took her off to the collecting ring. Rosie and Jess were already there, jumping back and forth over a couple of low jumps. They waved as Alex made his way over and the loudspeaker announced that the Open Jumping was starting.

Gently, Alex cantered a circle as the collecting ring emptied and riders made their way over to the ringside.

Alex slowed Puzzle to a walk. It wouldn't be long before Rosie took her turn at the course. Then there was a little wait till Jess and Izzy. Tom was next, Alex was after that, and Kate was the last competitor due in the ring. Slowly, Alex slid down from Puzzle's back and tied her up. He walked towards the ring, the gasps from the crowd indicating that the jumping was in full flow.

"Number 12, Cecily Griggs, four faults..." The loudspeaker was calling out.

A rider was cantering out of the ring, just as Alex found a place by the ringside.

"Rosie Edwards on Hector, riding for Sandy Lane Stables," boomed out over the loudspeaker.

Alex watched with interest. The bell sounded and Rosie cantered a neat circle before riding Hector to the first. They jumped cleanly over the brush and cantered towards the gate. Rosie leaned forward in the saddle and Hector rose to the challenge, landing neatly to ride up alongside the rails for the staircase. Cantering wide, they approached the sharks' teeth. Hector didn't hesitate, and now it was the triple bars. Alex counted their strides in the approach to the take-off... one, two, three... clear. Now the parallel bars. Over that and, as they cantered around the corner, the sound of pounding hooves filled the air. The crowd was quiet. Just three more jumps for a clear round. One... two... three... and they were sailing out of the ring. It had been a clear, steady round. Alex raised his eyebrows. Not bad, but he intended to go faster than that.

"Number 15, Rosie Edwards, jumping clear with no time faults," rang out over the loudspeaker.

The next rider was already thundering around the course as Alex made his way back to Puzzle.

"All right." He untied Puzzle's reins. "It's our turn soon. Let's show them."

Already the showjumping was up to the mid-twenties and the loudspeaker was announcing that there were four riders through to the jump-off. As Alex and Puzzle cantered over to the ring, Alex was greeted by a despondent looking Izzy coming out of the ring.

"Four faults," she muttered. "We overshot the parallel."

"Bad luck, Izzy." Alex tried to console her. "How did Jess do?"

"Disastrous." Izzy pulled a face. "Skylark was having one of her off-days. She knocked four jumps down."

"Oh dear..." Alex knew that wouldn't put Jess in a good mood. So there was only Rosie through to the jump-off so far.

Alex jumped down off Puzzle and tied her up to some wooden rails. Then he made his way over to the ring to find a place to watch. Ponies of all shapes and sizes thundered around the course before finally Tom and Chancey were announced. Alex watched his friend circle Chancey, waiting for the bell.

Chancey was hotting up, pawing at the ground. The crowd silenced and Tom rode Chancey for the first. They flew over the brush with feet to spare, and turned to the gate. They were going like the clappers, and this wasn't even being timed. Alex could tell they were going too fast, but it didn't look as though Tom had much say in the matter. The crowd was silent. Every snort that Chancey made echoed around the ring.

Now they were over the staircase. Chancey danced dangerously close to the sharks' teeth. Alex held his breath. Tom took it squarely, leaning forward in the saddle, but it was too late. As they sprang over the jump, Chancey clipped the back of it and the top bar came tumbling down.

"Ooh," the crowd groaned.

Tom drove Chancey at the centre of the triple bars and they cleared the jump and rode towards the parallel. They cleared that with ease and went on to

81

the treble. One... two.. three... jump... and they were cantering out of the ring. But it was no good. Chancey wasn't going to be through to the jump-off. Alex knew that Tom would be very disappointed.

"He fought me all the way." Tom looked as though he was putting a brave face on it as Alex came to greet him. "I'd better get him calmed down." And with that, Tom rode Chancey towards the trees.

Alex went to collect Puzzle, suddenly feeling nervous. With Tom out of the running, they had a real chance of winning. He hadn't felt this nervous about anything in ages – not even the county cricket trials had made him feel this way. Alex untied Puzzle's reins and cantered her across the grass to the collecting ring to practise a couple more jumps.

"Not long to go," he told her.

Alex cantered Puzzle over to the jumping ring to wait. It was their turn at last.

"Keep calm... keep calm." Alex leaned down to pat Puzzle's neck as the bell rang out and they cantered to the first jump. Deftly, Alex eased Puzzle over the brush and cantered her towards the gate. Puzzle sprang over the fence as if it were alight and Alex turned her for the staircase the minute they touched down. Clear of that, and Alex swung her wide for the sharks' teeth. He sat tight to the saddle, all of his concentration rooted on the fences in front of him. Alex was so light with his hands as they rode towards the middle of the next jump Puzzle could hardly have known he was there.

Carefully, Alex faced her at the triple bar and again

they glided over the jump with ease, swooping round in a large circle to take the parallel. Now it was only the treble. One... two... three... Touch down!

There was a loud cheer from the crowd as Alex and Puzzle cantered out of the ring. They had jumped clear! He clapped his hand to Puzzle's shoulder as they drew to a halt.

"Alex Hardy on Puzzle, jumping clear with no time faults... "

"Well done... well done, Alex," the Sandy Lane team called out as he trotted out of the ring.

Alex grinned. "We're through to the jump-off."

11

JUMP-OFF

The jumps in the ring were raised for the final round of the Open Jumping and the Sandy Lane riders stood by watching. There were eight riders through to the jump-off and this time the fastest clear round would win. Of the Sandy Lane riders, just Kate, Rosie and Alex had got through.

"Good luck you two," Alex muttered as they went off to collect their mounts.

One by one the riders took their turn at going into the ring and riding the course. When Rosie was called in fourth Alex went over to watch. Calmly, she turned into the ring for the second time and cantered forward for the brush. Clear of that, they rode to the gate. Hector's tail swished as she nudged him forward and they turned the corner for the staircase. Over that and onto the sharks' teeth. Hector flew over the jump and Rosie checked him, just in time for the triple bar. The jump took a bit of a rap and a hollow sound echoed around the ring, but it stayed up and now there was only the parallel and then the treble. The crowd held their breath as Rosie cleared the first jump and rode to the treble. One... two... three... touchdown. They were clear and a ripple of applause rang through the crowd.

"Great stuff, Rosie!" Alex called across as she cantered past him. It had been a safe round, putting her in third place. "It looks like it's me next." Alex gritted his teeth. Kate was still left to go after him. She and Feather had been training pretty hard. Could Puzzle really beat them? He'd have to go like the clappers to be in with a chance.

"Good luck," Jess and Kate called from behind the rails.

The crowd hushed as Alex circled his pony.

And then they were off... racing to the first as the clock began ticking its countdown. They sailed over the brush, and rode towards the gate. Soaring over that, they cantered towards the staircase. Puzzle's ears were pricked as she raced forward. All Alex could see were the fences ahead of him; all he could hear was the sound of pounding hooves as he rode to the triple bars. Alex put her at the middle of the jump, propelling Puzzle forward with his legs. She tucked her feet up under her as if the poles were hot pokers, and flew through the air.

Alex didn't even have time to think as he turned

her for the parallel. He steadied her in the approach and again they jumped clear. The moment they touched the ground, Alex turned her, so that there was hardly enough time for them to gather momentum. But he had judged it just right and Puzzle was clear, surging forward for the treble. One... two... three. Alex leaned forward in the saddle and the horse found her natural take-off. What a speed!

Alex could hardly contain himself. As he cantered through the finish, the voice from the speaker announced that he had taken the lead with a time of 55 seconds. Alex clapped his hand to Puzzle's neck in excitement.

"You were brilliant, Alex." Tom looked surprised as he called from the sidelines.

Alex shrugged. "I've still got Kate to beat." He frowned. It seemed mean to hope that his sister would do badly, but he couldn't help wishing she wouldn't be quite on top form.

"That was a pretty fast time, Alex. Well done," Nick said, coming over.

"Thanks," Alex turned a bit red and walked Puzzle towards the trees to cool down for the result.

It seemed to take forever as the loudspeaker called out the times and announced that Alex held the lead. Kate was in now. Alex didn't want to watch. He held his breath as the gasps echoed from the crowd. He could hardly bear to listen, and it was only when Kate rode out of the ring that he realized she hadn't gone as fast as him.

"Well done, Alex," Kate said graciously. "You're

still holding the lead."

"But there's still one more left to go in," he muttered.

Alex walked Puzzle a little way away. He couldn't bear to watch. It seemed to take forever for the last rider to complete the course but then he heard his name being called. His time hadn't been matched. He'd won!

The next thing Alex knew, he was cantering around the ring again, this time with a red rosette pinned to Puzzle's bridle and a huge silver cup in his hands. Beams of light sprang off it as it glinted in the sunlight and they galloped their lap of honour. As he rode out of the ring, he felt really proud. His friends were already standing by the entrance to the ring, ahead of him. Kate and Izzy raced over.

"Alex... Alex, you're not going to believe it," Kate cried. "Wow it's lovely," she said, stopping to look at the cup he was holding. "You've got to come over."

"What is it?" Alex asked.

"It's Puzzle," Kate said. "You're going to be really pleased. There are some people here who want to buy her, and guess what – they're offering £1,000! It's brilliant news, isn't it?"

Before Alex could say anything, Kate was rushing off. It *was* brilliant news, wasn't it? he thought, following on after her, Puzzle's reins hanging slackly by her neck. Alex was nearly at the oak tree now and he could see the Sandy Lane group ahead of him. There were a number of Sandy Lane riders talking to Nick and a man and a woman. They must be the people Kate had been talking about. Alex jumped to the ground and handed Puzzle's reins over to Kate.

"Alex. Well done!" Nick called. "Come over here. I've got some people I want you to meet. This is Mr. and Mrs. Norman – they've come down from the Midlands to check out the ponies at the show."

"We love your pony," the woman started, before Alex had even said hello. "She'd be perfect for our daughter."

"We didn't think she'd be for sale," the man joined in. "But Mr. Brooks explained you'd bought her as an investment. We'd be prepared to offer you £1,000."

Alex went red and before anyone could say anything more, he spoke out. "Look, I'm sorry, there's been a mistake. I've changed my mind. I'm afraid she's not for sale." And with that, he turned on his heel and walked away.

12

THE TRUTH IS OUT

No one was more taken aback than Alex by his reaction to the offer to buy Puzzle. After all, it was what he'd wanted – what he'd intended all along. Alex knew the others were pretty surprised, but no one said anything. Maybe it was the excitement after the show, or maybe they were embarrassed, but whatever the reason, Alex certainly wasn't going to bring the subject up.

As Alex groomed Puzzle on Monday morning, he thought about everything that had happened since Puzzle had arrived. He was miles away when Sarah's voice disturbed his thoughts.

"Puzzle did pretty well on Saturday, didn't she?" She leaned over Puzzle's stable door.

"Yes, yes she did," Alex answered.

"I'm going to come straight to the point," Sarah

said. "I asked Nick to talk to you, but I know he's been putting it off. We were under the impression that you were just stabling Puzzle here for the summer – not forever. I know you go back to school soon, so we need to know what your plans are. You're not likely to get a better offer than £1,000, you know."

"I know." Alex shrugged. "And I thought all along that I would sell her."

"And now?" Sarah questioned him.

"Well now I don't know that I want to. I think I want to keep her." It was the first time that Alex had admitted this to anyone and he was embarrassed.

"I can understand that," Sarah said gently. "You've worked so hard with her and she's come on such a lot. I didn't really believe that anyone would be able to get her properly well. If you've decided you do want to keep her, then you know we'd offer you first refusal on one of the boxes, only you would have to pay for it."

Alex looked despondent. "Yes, I know. I've been thinking about all of that and I don't know that I can afford a livery fee. I was wondering. I mean, would you be able to use her for lessons in return for her keep?"

"I don't want to sound mean," Sarah said. "But it won't be long now before our ponies are back in action, so we don't really need a spare pony."

Alex felt choked. "No, I guess not."

"If you want to keep her, why don't you talk to your parents and see what they say. They might help you out."

Alex opened his mouth. He was about to tell Sarah that his parents didn't even know about Puzzle, but then he thought better of it. Alex didn't say anything more. Sarah shrugged her shoulders and made her way across the yard to the cottage.

"Let me know what you decide, Alex," she called back.

"OK," Alex replied.

Talking to Sarah had set Alex thinking. Maybe it was about time he told his parents about Puzzle. After all, they'd certainly be pretty impressed when they heard what she was worth. But what would they say when he told them he wanted to keep her? Would they help him with a livery fee?

*

The long summer's day was drawing to a close as Alex cycled home. He'd been preparing what he was going to say to his parents, over and over in his head, but somehow the words didn't sound quite right.

As Alex propped his bike up against the wall of the mill, he walked into the kitchen, trying to look cheery in front of his mother.

"Where's Kate?"

"In the TV room," his mother answered him.

Quickly, Alex made his way down the corridor to find his sister.

"Ssh." She motioned towards the television as Alex

shut the door behind him.

"I've decided to tell Mum and Dad about Puzzle tonight." Alex blurted the words out.

Kate looked surprised as Alex went on to tell her how Sarah had offered him first refusal on a box and how he'd decided he was going to keep the pony. At the end of it, he looked up, expecting to see surprise on Kate's face, but her face looked pretty blank.

"Aren't you shocked?" Alex asked.

"Not really," Kate said. "Everyone's known for ages that you were really attached to Puzzle. We were just waiting for you to admit it."

"Oh..." Alex looked taken aback. "So what do you think Mum and Dad will say, do you think they'll help me out?"

"I don't know." Kate looked uncertain. "I guess they'll be pleased about the money she's worth, but as for asking them to pay a livery fee..."

"That's the problem, isn't it?" Alex looked thoughtful. "Now is as good a time as any to ask. Will you go and get Mum?"

Alex walked down the hallway towards the sitting room where his father was reading the paper.

"Dad, can I talk to you?" Alex started.

"Sure." Mr. Hardy looked up. "What's up? You look as though you've got the weight of the world on your shoulders."

At that point, Kate arrived with her mother in tow.

"What's going on?" Mrs. Hardy asked. Now that everyone was in the room, Mr. Hardy looked concerned. "What it it, Alex?"

Alex took a deep breath. "I've got something to tell you," he said, looking at his parents. "It's nothing to worry about. I guess it's good news in a way."

And before either of his parents could respond, Alex launched in.

"You know I've been trying to get the rest of the money for this cricket tour?" he started.

"Well yes," his father looked puzzled. "I know we said ages ago you could put your premium bond towards it, but we thought you'd gone off the idea. You haven't seemed so interested in the sport since you got dropped from the squad. We certainly haven't seen you doing anything about getting the extra £350."

"Well, I have in a way," Alex said. "You see, I had this great idea about how I could make the rest of the money – OK, so it's not quite the same sort of thing as Will or Jim are doing, but I thought it was pretty foolproof. You see, I thought that if I invested my £500 then I might be able to make the extra £350."

Mrs. Hardy groaned. "Oh Alex, we're not letting you invest your £500 in some mad scheme."

"No Mum, you're not getting me," Alex said quickly. "You see, I've already spent the £500. I've doubled my money. I bought a pony and now it's worth £1,000."

"WHAT?" his father exclaimed.

Alex looked at his parents' faces and saw their shocked expressions. Weren't they pleased that his investment had paid off?

"You see, they needed some more rideable ponies at Sandy Lane," Alex went on. "So I thought that if I bought one and lent it to them, they could use it, and I'd sell it on at the end of the summer."

"And the owners of the stables put you up to this, did they?" Mr. Hardy raised his eyebrows.

"No, no of course they didn't." Alex felt frustrated. "They didn't know anything about it till I turned up with the pony. Actually they weren't very pleased. She was a bit of a dud when I got her... but I nursed her back to health and Nick helped me train her and now she's brilliant... absolutely brilliant."

"You should see them together," Kate joined in. "They won the Open Jumping at Benbridge on Saturday."

"Let me get this straight," Mr. Hardy interrupted. "You've bought a pony, trained it up and didn't even think to tell us what you were doing?"

"Well, yes, I thought it would be better to tell you when it was all sorted," Alex explained, looking at their disappointed faces. "I guess I should have told you before," he hesitated. "Only I wanted to surprise you. But the situation's changed now... you see, I just want to keep her, and I was hoping you might help me out with a livery fee."

"A livery fee? So that's what this is all about," Mr. Hardy said. "You need money. What would you have done if you didn't need the money? Kept the secret from us forever?"

"No, no of course not," Alex said.

"And now you reckon this pony is worth £1,000, do you?" said Mr. Hardy, looking doubtful.

"Yes. That was the offer someone made at the

Benbridge Show," Alex said.

"And you'd rather keep this pony than sell her and go on the cricket tour?"

Alex hesitated. "Well yes, yes I would. I don't want to have to give the pony up."

"So is this why you haven't been making the cricket squad?" Mr. Hardy said.

"Oh, don't worry about that, I'll get my place back," Alex said confidently.

"Alex, I don't think you understand the seriousness of what you've just admitted," Mr. Hardy said calmly. "You went ahead and spent all your money on a pony. Now you say the gamble has paid off, which may or may not be the case, but you don't want to sell her. Well that's not an investment is it? It's irresponsible and what is worse, you did it all behind our backs. I'm disappointed in you, Alex."

"It wasn't like that," Alex broke in gruffly. "I didn't mean..."

Mr. Hardy held up his hand. "No Alex. No more excuses. You know you can't afford to keep a pony, and we really can't take this on at the moment. Ponies are a lot of work. I know what you're like. You'll get bored of it in no time at all and either Kate or your mother and I will be left to sort out your mess."

"But it's not like that, Dad," Alex cried.

"Isn't it?" Mr. Hardy frowned. "I think the best thing you can do is stick to your original plan. You bought this pony as an investment. Now you must sell it and put the money back where it came from."

"But Dad..." Alex looked as white as a sheet. He

knew that when his father had made his mind up about something, there would be no changing it. And that, it seemed, was the end of the discussion. Alex's father turned back to his newspaper and Alex was left standing there.

Alex left the room and closed the door behind him. It was only once he was alone in his bedroom that he stood with his back to the door, and let out a sigh. It was hopeless. He didn't have a choice. He would have to sell Puzzle.

13

A BRAVE FACE

As Alex cycled to Sandy Lane Stables the next morning, he felt terrible. Now that the business with Puzzle was all out in the open at home, he realized what a mess he'd made of everything. He needed to get everything off his chest and tell Nick and Sarah the whole truth too.

It was a perfect summer's day as Alex cycled down the dusty roads, but inside he felt less than perfect. He tried to look on the bright side of things – after all, wasn't this what he'd intended all along? Maybe he'd be able to get his place back in the cricket squad if he didn't have a pony to look after. It seemed ironic to think that the money he'd been offered for Puzzle would be more than enough to go on the tour. But somehow cricket didn't hold the same fascination now he was faced with the prospect of losing Puzzle forever. Cycling up the drive, Alex felt a cool breeze rustle through the trees.

"Hi Alex." Izzy called across as Alex drew to a halt. "I'm going to ride out to the beach. Do you fancy coming?"

"Um, I've got to talk to Nick first," Alex said, feeling unsettled. "But yeah, well that would be great."

"You'll catch him in the cottage," Izzy said breezily. "Sarah's taking a lesson in the outdoor school."

"Thanks," Alex muttered. He crossed the yard and made his way to the cottage. He knocked on the door and went inside.

"Oh, it's you, Alex." Nick looked up from a pile of papers. "I hear Sarah spoke to you yesterday about Puzzle's stabling."

"Yes, I don't know how to tell you this," Alex started. "And I know you're going to be pretty annoyed, but you see I never actually told my parents I'd bought a pony. You see, I'd bought her hoping to make a profit, and when she was a dead loss, I just didn't feel I could tell them."

Alex wasn't surprised when he looked up and saw how shocked Nick looked.

"I've told them everything now," Alex went on. "I had to if I was going to get any help with a livery fee. They were pretty cross that I had kept it from them. Anyway, Dad won't help me with a livery fee. He says I've got to sell Puzzle as soon as possible."

"I see," Nick started slowly. "I suppose I should

be pretty cross with you too, but I reckon you've been through enough already."

"You could say that," Alex said gratefully. "I've never seen my father look so disappointed since I got thrown out of the cubs." He tried to make a joke out of an awkward situation.

"And is your father sure about this?" Nick said slowly.

"Very sure," Alex said despondently. "When he's made up his mind over something he doesn't change it. I was going to ask if you might try and sell her for me. I don't care so much about the price – I want her to go to a good home."

"I'll see what I can do," Nick said. "I doubt you'll get another offer like the one you had at the Benbridge Show, but you have done wonders with her, so it shouldn't be a problem selling her."

"All right." Alex started towards the door. "Oh, and Nick," he turned back, "do you think you could keep this quiet for the moment? I don't want the others knowing and feeling sorry for me."

"I understand," Nick said.

"Thanks," Alex replied. "I'm going for a beach ride with Izzy if you want me."

"OK," Nick said.

Alex closed the door behind him. He took a deep breath and stepped out of the cottage. He could see Izzy's head just inside Midnight's stable.

"Are you ready?" Alex called across to her, trying to sound as normal as possible.

"Sure," Izzy called back. "Midnight's raring to go."

"I'll be right with you." Alex forced a smile as he made his way over to Puzzle. It was only once he was in the safety of her stable that he stopped for a minute and let down his guard. "Oh Puzzle. If only you knew," he groaned as he rested his head on the little pony's chestnut neck.

Puzzle shook her red-brown mane and impatiently nudged at his chest.

"All right... all right. I know you're anxious to go out for a ride," he said, setting to work with a body brush.

Soon he had given her a quick clean and set about tacking her up.

"Come on," he muttered, leading Puzzle out of the yard and springing up onto her back.

As he and Izzy started to make their way out of the yard, he heard Kate's excited voice behind him.

"Alex... Alex," she called as she cycled into the yard.

Izzy was already through the back gate and cantering off across the fields. Alex took a deep breath and quickly followed on after Izzy, pretending he hadn't heard Kate's call. He felt a bit guilty, but right now he really didn't want to talk about Puzzle any more. A decision had been made, and nothing could change that.

As the wind rushed past him, Alex immersed himself in his riding. They cantered across the fields, and soon they were approaching the scrubland that led to the beach.

"Race you to the sands," Izzy cried.

Izzy had a head start but as Alex nudged Puzzle into a gallop, they soon caught her up. The two riders drew to a halt at the top of the cliffs and looked down onto the beach below. The sea was choppy and white-crested waves crashed down onto the sands.

"Come on, let's go down," Alex cried. He couldn't wait to get onto the beach and race alongside the sea. If that wouldn't take his mind off things, he didn't think anything could.

*

As Izzy and Alex returned from the beach, trotting into the yard, Alex found a rather cross-looking Kate ahead of him.

"I'll catch you later, Izzy," he called, riding Puzzle over to where Kate was sitting on the gate. Alex could see from the determined expression on her face that she was fuming.

"All right?" he asked.

"No, I'm not all right," she snapped. "There you go, rushing off at the crack of dawn this morning. And then I get to Sandy Lane and you pretend you don't even hear me."

"OK, OK, I'm sorry," Alex answered. "It's just that I didn't want to talk any more. I spoke to Nick and he's going to look for a home for Puzzle."

"So it's all going ahead then?" Kate said miserably. "I sort of hoped that Nick might be able to do something about it."

Alex frowned. "He's got a business to run, hasn't he? Anyway, I don't want to talk about it any more. I want to keep it to myself for the moment, so don't go blabbing to the others, will you?"

"OK, keep you hair on," Kate answered in a hurt voice as Alex jumped down from Puzzle's back and led her off, the reins trailing by her side.

14

BORROWED TIME

Time passed quickly over the next couple of days. If Alex hadn't known better, he could almost have believed he hadn't had the conversation with his parents and that Puzzle wasn't really going to be sold.

He'd gone back and told his parents that Nick was looking for a buyer for Puzzle and that, it seemed, was that. The subject was closed. His parents said nothing more and Alex didn't want to talk about it. By blocking it out of his mind, he could at least enjoy the last few days of the summer holidays with Puzzle.

When Nick called Alex to the cottage on Thursday morning, he knew exactly what Nick was going to say.

"You've found her a home, haven't you?" Alex pre-empted Nick's words.

"Well, yes. Yes I have," Nick said. "It's a good

one. She can go almost immediately."

"When's immediately?" Alex burst out.

"Sunday," Nick answered. "I know you're back at school on Monday, so I thought it would probably be all right, but I said I'd check with you first."

Alex nodded gloomily.

"The buyers came over to the yard last night," Nick went on. "I thought it might be best if you weren't here while they inspected her in case it came to nothing, but they liked her. Actually, they saw you ride at the Benbridge Show, and that was what did it for them."

Alex's heart tightened in his chest. "Well, I guess that's it then. Time to say goodbye."

"Good lad," Nick said. "They're offering £850 for her as well which should be a bit of a sweetener."

Alex shrugged. It was exactly the amount he'd needed for the cricket tour.

"So that's all right?" Nick questioned.

"I guess so," Alex answered.

"OK then, I'll give these people a ring and let them know that you've agreed," Nick said.

"Thanks Nick," Alex said, a lump rising in his throat. "It really is a good home, is it?"

"It's the best," Nick answered him. "They live over by Walbrook. They've got acres of fields, and the girl who wants her is keen to compete on the show circuit too. I've already spoken to your parents about this, by the way. I gave them a ring last night."

"My parents?" Alex was speechless. He'd been out at the cinema, but he would have thought they'd have mentioned it when he got in. "But why? Why did you call them?"

"Well," Nick hesitated. "I wanted to tell them that I'd found a buyer, but I also thought they should know what a good job you'd done on getting Puzzle fit and healthy. Your Dad did say he knew you were having a hard time right now and that he was proud of the way you'd seen sense and agreed to let Puzzle go."

"I suppose that's something," Alex reflected. "Thanks Nick."

*

Now that Alex knew for certain that Puzzle was going, he decided it was only fair to let everyone else know at the yard. All the regulars had become pretty attached to Puzzle and Alex found it hard to cope with all their sympathy. But if Alex was going to get through these last few days at Sandy Lane, he knew there was only one way to do it. He had to put Sunday out of his mind and concentrate on the present. He had to enjoy being with Puzzle and block everything else from his mind.

When he and Puzzle cantered around the outdoor school that morning, he tried hard to ignore the sadness that felt like a real pain in his chest. As they rode around the course of jumps, clearing them with ease, Alex shut everything out of his mind. As he settled down to bring Puzzle to a halt, he heard someone clapping from the side of the rails. Tom was standing there, holding Chancey by the reins.

"Pretty good," he called. "You should be proud of her."

"I am." Alex adjusted his riding hat.

"Mind if Chancey and I join you?" Tom asked. "We could do with the practice."

"Sure," Alex replied.

Quickly Tom loosened Chancey up over a couple of practice jumps, and then they were ready to take the course.

Alex waited for Tom to jump the first two jumps and then he followed him, matching him stride for stride. They soared over the brush and cantered towards the sharks' teeth. Puzzle jumped her heart out and, as they sailed over the wall and cantered a circuit around the school, Alex could almost believe the light-headed feeling would go on and on forever.

15

GOODBYE PUZZLE

Before Alex knew it, the sun was waking him through the curtains on Sunday morning. The awful day that he'd been trying to pretend would never come, was here.

Kate didn't say much to him when he came down the stairs for breakfast that morning. She looked as gloomy as Alex felt, but Alex knew he couldn't show it. He had already decided that the only way he could get through today was to treat it as if everything was normal. He intended to muck Puzzle out, feed her, groom her, take her for a ride – just as he had done every day of the summer holidays.

As Alex cycled along the roads that morning, his heart felt heavy. It was quiet when he turned up the drive to Sandy Lane and cycled into the yard. Puzzle was being picked up at eleven, so there would just be enough time for a quick ride out to Larkfield Copse and back.

Vaguely, Alex wondered why Nick wasn't up and about. He was normally in the yard at the crack of dawn, and this was Puzzle's last day after all. Still... Nick had seen lots of horses come and go. This was probably just business as usual for him.

Despondently, Alex brushed Puzzle's coat. He hadn't waited for Kate that morning. He hadn't known how to explain to her that he just wanted to be on his own with Puzzle. Somehow it sounded silly.

Alex wiped Puzzle's coat with a soft cloth, polishing her until her red-brown coat gleamed. Then he turned and made his way to the tack room to collect her saddle and bridle. It was going to be a lovely day and, as he tacked Puzzle up and led her out of her stable, he tried to cheer up. He wanted to make the most of this last ride. Opening the back gate, he sprang up into the saddle and rode across the first field in the direction of Larkfield Copse.

Gradually, Alex forgot himself in his riding as they cantered across the grass. Lightly he touched Puzzle with his heels and she stretched out into a gallop. Alex's face felt taut as the wind whistled past and he fed the reins up Puzzle's neck, stretching out her stride. He'd never forget the time he'd had with Puzzle... never, he told himself. She'd taught him such a lot – without her he'd never have realized what he was missing out on by not riding. From now on he was going to appreciate being down at Sandy Lane a whole lot more.

Alex looked at his watch. It was ten thirty. He'd have to get a move on if he was going to be back at the yard in time. And so Alex turned Puzzle and made his way across the fields. As he rode through the surrounding countryside, he tried to get a grip of himself. This was for the best... the best for everyone.

Now there was only one more field to cross. Desperately, Alex hoped he'd be able to keep his cool in front of everyone.

As he trotted down the lane between the fields and rounded the corner to the yard, Alex prepared himself for the mass of faces that would be there to greet him. He dismounted and unlatched the back gate, leading Puzzle forward.

He'd been right – the yard was busy – there stood Izzy, Tom, Rosie, Jess, Kate and... his dad! What on earth was he doing at Sandy Lane? Slowly, Alex led Puzzle over to where his father stood.

"What are you doing here?" He stumbled over the words and then, realizing that his tone sounded rather rude, he started again. "I mean, you do know this is Puzzle's last day here, don't you?"

And now Nick appeared behind his father, smiling broadly. Had everyone gone mad?

"I don't know what you're all staring at, but I've got a pony to get ready," Alex said crossly, leading Puzzle off.

"Alex... just wait a minute." Nick grabbed hold of his shoulder. "I think you should listen to what your father has to say."

Alex stood quite still, looking bemused.

"Puzzle's not going today," Nick stepped in.

"What?" Alex looked from Nick to his dad and now everyone had gathered around, petting Puzzle. What was going on?

"I phoned the people who wanted to buy her," Nick explained. "I've told them she's not for sale after all. Actually I've found a nice little black Arab for them on the other side of Walbrook, so they're quite happy."

"Are you mad?" Alex tied Puzzle to a ring in the wall and stepped over, looking from Nick to his father "I'm back at school on Monday and you said it was a good home."

"And so it would have been," Nick said. "Only I think Puzzle will be better off at Sandy Lane. Shall I continue – or would you like to fill him in on the details?" He turned to Mr. Hardy.

"Well Alex," his father started. "We've decided you can keep the pony. She's yours. I'll pay a livery fee."

"What? What do you mean?" Alex could hardly contain his excitement. "You were so adamant that you wouldn't help."

"I know, but I've changed my mind and – well, she's not going to be *all* yours anyway," his father started before Alex could interrupt. "There is a condition attached."

Alex looked wary but his father was quick to go on. "I want you to share her with your sister."

"With Kate? Is that it?" Alex couldn't believe his ears. "Of course I'll share Puzzle with her. But why didn't you tell me any of this before? Why did you make me think I was going to lose her?"

"I suppose seeing how you looked when you thought you would lose her made me realize you should keep her," his father said. "Nick phoned and told us how awful you felt that you'd disappointed us and how you hoped that by selling her it would make things better. Well I suppose that was when I realized that enough was enough. You've learned your lesson, Alex."

"Phew," Alex said. It was a lot to take in. And then Alex's face fell.

"What is it?" his father asked. "You do still want the pony, don't you?"

"Of course I want her!" Alex laughed. "It's just that I'd got it into my head that I'd be able to pay off all my debts. I still owe Kate a tenner from the sale and then I had to borrow £50 for the vet's bills."

"Well, you can take that out of your savings account now," his father said.

Alex looked blankly at him. Didn't his father know he'd spent all of his money on Puzzle?

"I've told your mother I'll put half of the money back into your savings account," his father explained. "It's only fair if you're sharing the pony with Kate. Of course this does mean you won't have the money to go on this cricket tour."

"I don't care about that now. There'll be other tours. I can't believe it! I just don't know what to say. Except, that's absolutely brilliant, and thank you."

"Great! So it looks like you might be spending

more time at Sandy Lane after all," Izzy stepped in.

"Yeah, I guess so," Alex muttered, turning red.

And at that moment, there was a loud whinny that broke up the awkward conversation. It was Puzzle. In all of the excitement, Alex had forgotten that he'd left her tied to a ring on the wall.

"All right... all right, I'm coming," he said, running over and leading her over. "I think you'd better come and meet Dad."

And as the riders stood there, talking away, Alex stood back from the group. Who'd have thought he'd ever have felt so at one with a pony? He and Puzzle really were the perfect team. Alex looked at his pony – her coat was shiny, her eyes gleamed and her ears were pricked. She looked just as good as any other pony... better than any other pony, for she was just right for him. She was better than just right. She was perfect.

Strangers at the Stables by Michelle Bates

The third title in the Sandy Lane Stables series

...Thoughts jostled around in Rosie's mind as she crossed the yard. She couldn't believe how many things had gone wrong in the couple of weeks Nick and Sarah had been gone. She needed time to think. There was something worrying her, right at the back of her mind... something that held the key to it all. But what was it?

When the owners of Sandy Lane are called away, everyone still expects the stables to run smoothly in their absence. No one is quite prepared for all the things that happen over the next few weeks. There isn't time to get help, the children of Sandy Lane have to act fast, if they want to save their stables...

The Midnight Horse by Michelle Bates

The fourth title in the Sandy Lane Stables series

The horse cantered gracefully around
the paddock in long easy strides, his tail
held high, the crest of his neck arched.
His jet-black coat contrasted sharply
with the white frost, his hooves hardly
seemed to touch the ground as he danced
forward.

Riding at the Hawthorn Horse Trials is all that Kate
has dreamed of and this year she's in with a real
chance of winning. As she works hard to prepare for
the day, it seems nothing will distract her from her
goal. But then the mysterious midnight horse rides
into Kate's life, and suddenly everything changes...

Ride by Moonlight by Michelle Bates

The sixth title in the Sandy Lane Stables series

The ground started spinning. Charlie's head was reeling. He felt as though he was seeing everything double. He couldn't think. He couldn't stop thinking. His mind was in a whirl as everything came flooding back – the high-pitched whinny, the thundering hooves, the crashing fall – all echoed around his head...

When Charlie loses his nerve in a riding accident, no one thinks for a moment it'll be long before he's back in the saddle. But as the weeks go by, his friends begin to realize it's going to take something quite exceptional to get him riding again...

Horse in Danger by Michelle Bates

The seventh title in the Sandy Lane Stables series

Rosie couldn't see anything, yet she could definitely *hear* something. The stable in the far corner of the yard was shut, both sections of the door bolted tightly to a close. Rosie didn't know why, but suddenly she felt very nervous.

Taking a deep breath, she crossed the yard and pulled back the bolt on the door. As she slid it open, a hand plunged forward and grabbed her into the darkness...

Rosie and Jess have always been the greatest of friends, but more recently they've found themselves drifting apart. On the Autumn Treasure Hunt Ride, Rosie sets out to make amends. But what she discovers that day takes her down a path of deception and danger, putting her friendship with Jess to the ultimate test.